NAIVE TO THE STREETS

A. Roy Milligan

Copyright © 2020 by A. Roy Milligan

ISBN: 978-0-9969511-1-1

All rights reserved. No part of this book may be reproduced or transmitted in any form or by any means, electronic or mechanical, including

Photocopying, recording, or by any information storage and retrieval system, without permission in writing from the copyright owner.

This is a work of fiction. Names, characters, places and incidents either are the product of the author's imagination or are used fictitiously, and any resemblance to any actual persons, living or dead, events, or locales is entirely coincidental. This book was printed in the United States of America.

CHAPTER 1

Triangle was inside the steaming hot shower for an hour now, washing all the filth off her body from all the men she had sex with last night. She gave up her body as a favor for Ant, a guy who claimed he loved her.

"Triangle!" Ant yelled. "Come here! How long you gon' be in that shower?"

Ant and Triangle had been messing around with each other for a year now. It started off with just her and him having sex, but soon he realized he was able to take advantage of her in a way she never saw coming. Ant stood 6'4" tall, 250 pounds, dark skin with long dreads that nearly touched his back. Triangle on the other hand was 5'5" tall and maybe weighed 147 pounds soaking wet. She was a rare mix of black, white and Mexican, she definitely had no problem getting a guy's attention. People always said she looked like the actress Lauren London.

Triangle walked out of the bathroom five minutes later and entered the kitchen where Ant was sitting at the counter, drinking a forty. To her dismay, she saw three other guys sitting on the sectional white couch in the living room. She hoped Ant didn't want her to do what she was thinking. She was still tired and a little sore from last night, not to mention she didn't get much sleep. She stared at the guys for a second then looked back at Ant. She had never seen these guys before. "What Ant?"

Ant had a serious look on his face and Triangle thought for a second that he might hit her, but right now that would be better than having sex.

"Bitch, what you mean, what? I have been calling yo' dumb ass for 20 minutes!" he yelled, as he slightly turned red and his right fist clenched up with three gold rings glaring back at her. "You got my niggas waiting all damn day like you somebody important or something. Do that shit again and I will break yo' fucking neck," he told her and meant it. His big chain dangled from his pit bull sized neck and swung loosely in front of his white wife beater.

"Ok, I'm sorry baby! I had to clean myself up. What you need?" she asked with a softer tone of voice.

"I need you to fuck and suck these nigga's for me. Gon' ahead and let them see how good that pussy is," he told her, looking over at the three men with a smile on his face.

This was nothing new, Ant always had new guys over to fuck Triangle. "When? Right now?" she asked, hoping and praying that he would say no.

"Yeah! I'ma hit that shit first though, then you can let them do whatever they want! You got that?"

Triangle put her head down in complete submission and said, "Yes, I got it!" She had been feeling like an unpaid prostitute for about a month now. Ever since Ant had lost his job at the plant because of a major round of layoffs, money had been tight. He was also selling weed, but there was a shortage of that right now. He couldn't find any good weed anywhere, unless he was willing to drive out of town to get it himself and that wasn't an option for him. He wasn't about to be driving all over with large quantities of weed. Since Triangle had been staying at his house every weekend, she had been his money maker, sleeping with as many dudes as Ant could find.

"Where Sincere Meagan Good looking ass at?" Ant asked, testing her to see if Triangle was mad or not.

"She at home, I think."

Ant could tell she had a little attitude, but he didn't care, he needed the money.

"I thought you was gonna get her to give me some pussy. What you think, I just been letting you drive my van for free?" Ant asked her, making her feel like shit.

"So, I'm not good enough for you? Why you want to fuck my friend?" she asked with her arms crossed over her chest.

CHAPTER 2

"You fuck my friends," he said with a lecherous look on his face. "Why can't I fuck yours?"

"I tried, but she not like that. I'll try to find you another girl."

"Naw, I want Sincere," he said knowing it was pissing her off. For some reason, he liked pissing her off. She put up with it because she wanted to drive his van, although it was ancient and rusted, it offered her freedom of sorts. It was an old beige and brown van he had for years now. He didn't even care about the van. He had retagged it and put it in a person's name that wasn't even living anymore. He only used the van to get what he wanted from Triangle. He knew by giving her a vehicle at the age of 17, he could have her doing any and everything he asked. She didn't have a job or license, so she came to Ant for everything. He would barely give her pennies even though he was making hundreds off her ass every day. His plan had been working for about a month now and he had no plans on stopping, no matter how often he told her it was only for a little while longer.

Triangle became mad and she was ready to just have sex with them so she could leave. It was Sunday and she had been giving up the pussy since Friday, but being in Flint was a getaway for her every time she felt like being someplace where no one knew who she was.

Triangle stood there thinking for a moment whether Ant loved her or not. "Well come on, let's get this over with, I don't have all day!" she said, turning away from Ant and walking into the bedroom. Her sweet ass swayed from left to right and all the men followed her with their eyes and hardened dicks.

"Damn my dick is already leaking!" one guy said from behind, not taking his eyes off of her.

"Hell yeah, Ant hooked that shit up," another guy said, slapping Ant on the shoulder, giving him mad props.

"See nigga, I told you she was a bad muthafucka'. I only deal with bad ass bitches. And she got some good pussy too. Wait until you hit that muthafucka', you gonna be ready to take her home with you, watch and see," Ant bragged as they entered the bedroom.

Triangle heard all the comments and that was the one thing she loved. Ant would always make her feel special and talk good about her. Triangle just smiled to herself. She knew she was beautiful and she knew that most guys were attracted to her body. She had also been told by some guys that they wished she was older, back when she was just a few years younger. She had been on her own for some time now and had been lying about her age for years, because of the body she had. Her booty was big and round and it stuck out. She had wide hips and a small waist.

Triangle wasn't in contact with her mother, but she knew she was somewhere, homeless in Detroit which was only about an hour away from Flint. Her mom had been on drugs most of Triangle's life and she was now at the point where she sometimes told people that her mom was dead. She had no clue who her father was and she never bothered trying to find him and it seemed like he wasn't trying to find her either. When people asked Triangle who her father was, she would answer by saying, "The Streets." She had been surviving in the streets for so long she could care less about what someone had to say about her. She was getting by the best way she knew how. Triangle doubted her mom even knew who her father was anyways.

Soon, everyone was standing inside a bright room that looked like a motel room or a set from a porno. A bed sat in the middle of the room, with two night stands on each side. The night stands were made of a light colored wood and matched the headboard and footboard of the bed. There was a dresser to the left with a mirror attached to the wall. The carpet was a cream color and looked freshly vacuumed.

CHAPTER 3

Triangle began to slowly undress, like a strip tease, starting with her canary-yellow booty shorts and slung them over by the flat screen that hung on the wall. The shorts caught the corner of the TV and dangled erotically from the side. Since she wasn't wearing any panties, the only thing she had left to take off was her shirt. She looked around and saw four pair of eyes were locked on her like a radar. All the men were drooling and licking their lips like they were about to devour a steak. They couldn't wait to have a piece of her. Her only comfort was Ant being there with her. She knew that Ant wouldn't let anyone hurt her.

Her white halter top came flying off next and she threw it at the crowd and climbed on all fours onto the bed, and looked back at Ant. Her pussy was cleanly shaved and she had those hanging lips looking right at him.

"Come on Ant, you first right?" she asked, swinging her long hair from one side of her head to the other.

"Hell yeah," Ant replied, quickly pulling down his black shorts and boxers that read "BIG DADDY" on them. He

NAIVE TO THE STREETS |A. ROY MILLIGAN

climbed in the bed with her and stuck his dick in from behind.

"Ohh shit," she moaned, throwing her ass back onto his dick. The other guys watched the action for about five minutes before they started getting undressed to join in. One guy, with a tattoo on his neck of a scorpion, inserted his dick into her mouth while Ant was busy banging away at her pussy. Another stuck his finger in and out of her ass with a finger that needed the nail trimmed, while the third guy watched as he stroked his dick, waiting for a hole to open up. Ant kept hitting her pussy, then he pulled out and grabbed her hair to turn her face around. When she spit the dick out that was already in her mouth, Ant busted his nut directly in her mouth.

"Naw man, fuck that! Why would you bust in her mouth? I'm trying to get my dick sucked next and I don't want your fluids on my shit!" one guy complained to Ant. His name was Brian and he was about the same size as Ant, but light skinned, with tight corn rows.

"Fuck you man! I always bust in her mouth, besides, this my bitch!" Ant yelled back, reminding him of whose girl she was, as he pulled his shorts back on.

"Man, I aint paying for this shit! This shit nasty! I want my $500 back! I'll go find another hoe," Brian said, holding his hand out for his money back.

"Come on Brian, come hit this pussy, we straight," one of the other guys said as he inserted his dick into Triangle's pussy, not caring about fluids or anything else but getting it in.

"Man fuck that! I want my money back," Brian yelled, walking over to Ant.

"Ain't no refunds going on over here bro," Ant said, grabbing the gun that was under the bed. It was a small, yet a powerful chrome pistol. Triangle was still getting the shit fucked out of her while Ant and Brian were arguing. She was shocked that Ant was charging them $500 a piece to fuck her. She kept fucking because she thought maybe this time Ant would give her some of the cash he was making today. She started moaning louder to cover the sounds of the argument until Ant said, "Shut the fuck up, bitch!"

"Naw, you shut the fuck up and pay me my money!" Brian demanded, tired of arguing. He pulled up his sweat pants and put his Nike shoes on, ready to take his shit back.

"Fuck you and your money! You not getting shit, a deal is a deal!"

"Oh yeah?" Brian said, with fire in his eyes, ready to charge at Ant.

"Yea nigga', that's right!" Ant told him, pulling the gun out that he had hidden by his side.

Triangle's eyes turned towards Ant and she could see it was getting serious. It became hard for her to enjoy the sex, but the guy behind her was steady stroking in and out of her, not missing a beat. "Wait! Wait!" she finally said, jumping off the bed. "Please Ant, don't do this."

"Don't worry shorty, he ain't gonna do shit with that pistol," Brian said with confidence.

CHAPTER 4

"Get the fuck outta my house!" Ant yelled, pointing the gun at Brian. Triangle jumped in the middle of them, butt ass naked and the other two guys hurried up and put their clothes on.

"I ain't going nowhere until I get my $500. I'm either leaving with this bitch or you gonna pay me in cash, I'm sure I can make more off her anyway," Brian said, clenching and unclenching his fists.

"Nigga, you got ten seconds to get outta my house or...," Ant started to say before Brian cut him off.

"Or what? What the fuck you gonna do with all these witnesses here? You ain't stupid. Now YOU got ten seconds to give me my $500 or I'm about to kick your ass and this nasty bitch ass!" Brian said, pointing at Triangle who was facing Ant.

"Who you calling a bitch?" Triangle asked, turning around to face Brian. Her hair was like a whip as it spun around her head.

"You bitch!" Brian replied, ducking out of the way of her hair.

"Bitch, finish fucking and stay the fuck out of my business," Ant said to her as he pushed her roughly onto the stained sheets of the bed.

Seconds later, Brian came charging across the room and Ant let off a number of shots, first dropping Brian with a shot to the throat, blood sprayed out like it was coming from a paint gun. Then Ant turned the gun on the other two guys and dropped them to the floor. One bullet went through the side of one guy's mouth, hitting a tooth and ricocheting through the back of his skull, the other shot went in and out the side of the third guy's watermelon shaped head and ended up going through the headboard before finally finding a home in the drywall.

Triangle's stomach dropped, her brain froze and she felt numb. It was like she wanted to scream and run, but she couldn't. All she could think of was being shot next. She just sat on the bed like a rag doll and stared into Ant's eyes as he was holding the gun. The room was silent and instead of smelling like sex, the odor of gun powder filled the room.

"We gotta get them out of here," Ant said, breaking the deadly silence.

"W..We?" she stuttered out, on the verge of crying, but scared to.

"Yeah we! We gotta get them outta here, come on!" Ant said, seriously. "Put on your clothes and hurry up," he said as he wrapped the bodies up in the sheets and started dragging the bodies out, one by one.

Triangle was still in shock and was moving slowly to put her clothes on. She did not want to be near the bodies, let alone touch them. She was shaking uncontrollably and felt like she had to throw up. In her head she was thinking of how she was going to get away from Ant's crazy ass. She knew he wasn't about to just let her walk away so easily. By the time Ant came in for the next body, she had put her shorts and shirt on.

"Oh, I see you don't want to help, it's cool. Don't worry about it. Stay right here until I come back! Start cleaning some of this blood up, there's carpet cleaner in the closet. When I come back, there are some things we need to talk about and get straight."

"O...ok," Triangle said, sitting down on the bed trying to stop from passing out. She couldn't help but stare at Brian's body. Blood was still pumping out of his neck and she felt his eyes staring at her, accusing her, as if she had shot him. She watched Ant struggle with Brian's dead body. She wasn't sure what he was doing with the bodies, but she didn't care, she was just ready to leave. She got down on her hands and knees after getting the gallon container of carpet cleaner. Then she began cleaning the carpet the best she could while holding down the deluge of vomit that threatened to expel from her mouth. She was still shaking, for what seemed like hours, but in reality it was a mere twenty minutes. Finally Ant walked in and closed the door behind him. His skin was lathered in sweat and he was breathing hard, like he had just ran a marathon. He put all the bodies in the van Triangle would be driving away in.

"Look here Triangle... you tell anyone about this shit, I'ma kill you bitch. I hope you believe that and be smart about the situation," Ant told her.

CHAPTER 5

"I will… I won't tell anyone, I swear," she said looking at him seriously believing he would kill her as easy as he killed them.

"How do I know you won't? What if they charge you with murder? Would you do life?"

"Yes Ant, I will do life for you," She said, now regretting she didn't jump out the window before he came back in.

"I don't believe you bitch!" he said calmly while slapping her off the bed and onto the still wet floor. Even though she scrubbed the carpet, a pinkish stain still told the story. Brian's blood was sprayed across the flat screen TV, looking like a scene out of a horror film.

"Stopppp!" she screamed, while Ant repeatedly punched her in the face, stomach, and back. He beat her for three long minutes, kicking and stomping her until she stopped screaming. She was in too much pain to fight back. She was no match for a man his size. When he was done, Triangle was no longer moving. Ant barely blinked in the process of beating her. Somewhere, the psychopathic switch had been turned on inside his head, making it a normal thing that didn't bother him in the least.

"Get yo' ass up bitch!" Ant screamed, while giving her another kick into the chest with his running shoe. Her eyes flickered open. He had knocked her out, but with this last kick, he woke her back up. Ant could see treads of his shoes imprinted on her white shirt.

"P.l..e.ase," she whispered, with a mouth full of blood. She lay there, bleeding onto the carpet she had just scrubbed, feeling like she was about to die.

"Now… you gonna keep that mouth shut?" Ant asked, switching back to the nice guy, now that he was satisfied with the lesson he had just taught her.

"Y..e..s," she said, barely able to form the words from her voice box.

Ant still didn't believe her and he wanted to kill her. "Get up and get yourself together." he said, as he watched her get off the floor. It took her almost ten minutes to get herself up while Ant just sat on the bed watching her with his murdering eyes. When she finally made it to her feet, she held her arm across her stomach because the pain to her ribs was so excruciating. Looking in the mirror she could see her left eye was swollen, and her lip was busted. As she hobbled to the sink in the bathroom she thought her ankle was almost broke. Ant just stared at her, wondering if she would really turn him in.

"Finish cleaning yourself up, we need to get out of here before someone calls the cops about hearing shots being fired in here," Ant told her, going into the living room to look out the door.

Triangle didn't say anything, she just limped into the shower and changed clothes. When she was done, she obediently went to find Ant for her next instructions, wearing a pair of faded jeans and a long sleeve shirt to hide the bruising on her arms and legs.

"OK. Listen, I'm gonna go out of town for a while, I'ma leave you with the van while I'm gone. I'll call you when I get back then you can come over, but until then you stay away from this house, you got that?" Ant told her, making sure she understood what was at stake.

"Yes, I understand Ant! How long will you be gone?" Triangle asked him, having a hard time breathing without being in pain.

"Don't worry about me. You're free to go… and remember, keep your fucking mouth shut or you'll wind up just like them niggas!"

Triangle nodded her head up and down and walked out the front door. She was relieved to be out of that house. She half expected a bullet in her back as she walked outside. She nearly ran to the van and got inside, locking the doors. As soon as the van started, she drove off, aware of Ant watching her out the window until she was out of sight. As soon as she was down the street she grabbed her cell phone and called Sincere.

"Hello?" Sincere answered.

"Sincere," Triangle said, her voice was full of tears.

"What girl, whats wrong?"

"I need to talk to you. I'm coming to get you ok?" Triangle asked her, hoping she wasn't busy with nothing important.

Sincere didn't answer right away and then asked, "When right now?"

"Yes, I'm on my way. I'm leaving Flint right now. I'll be there in about 30 minutes."

"Okay," Sincere replied. She could hear the tears in Triangle's voice, but she had no idea what was going on. Even though she was doing her homework, she was gonna be there for her girl like always.

CHAPTER 6

"Dad, Triangle is on her way over here!" Sincere yelled, closing her Humanities text book. Sincere knew that her dad didn't want her around Triangle, but she always tried to convince him to change his mind.

"Yeah okay. Better yet… Never mind, she alright?" he said, not even bothering to tell her again that Triangle was heading down a rough road.

"What dad?"

"Nothing, it's nothing!"

"Yes it is something. What were you gonna say?" Sincere asked, pressing him for an answer.

Sincere's dad was a drug dealer, so he didn't like much company over, especially Sincere's friend Triangle. Her dad thought she was a sneaky, bad girl, but Sincere always tried to tell him positive things about her.

"Has that girl got her license yet?" he asked her when he heard a knock on the door. Saved by the knock from saying what was really on his mind, he asked, "Who is it?"

"Triangle," came the voice from the other side of the door.

Sincere's dad let Triangle in and immediately he was taken back by her swollen and beaten face. "What happened to you?" he asked, waving for her to come inside. Triangle couldn't say a word, she just burst into tears. "Calm down. Sincere, come here!" he yelled, as Sincere came running down the stairs, wearing a red button up shirt and a pair of denim shorts.

"Oh my god! What happened Tri?" Sincere asked, running into the kitchen to get some ice and a wet cloth for her friend.

Triangle wanted to tell her what happened, but fear wouldn't let her tell the truth, plus she knew Sincere's dad already didn't like her. "I got jumped by five girls at the gas station."

Sincere was pissed instantly and she was ready to throw down, "What girls?"

"I don't know them, they just came out of nowhere and took my purse with all my money in it," Triangle said, still in tears.

"You want me to call the police or an ambulance?" Sincere asked.

"No!" Triangle and Sincere's dad yelled out at the same time, both for their own reasons.

"Well, I'ma leave you two alone, I gotta be somewhere in twenty minutes, so Sincere I will see you later baby." Sincere's dad said as he lovingly kissed her on the forehead.

"Triangle, you gonna be okay lil lady?" he asked with fatherly concern.

"Yes I'll be fine, thanks!"

"Sincere call me if you decide to leave okay? Help her get cleaned up!" Sincere's daddy was a monster of a dude, easily weighing over 300 lbs. His closest friends called him Tiny which was absurd because there was nothing tiny about him. He drove a black Hummer with purple running lights, the only vehicle he could comfortably fit inside of.

"Okay daddy, I will," Sincere said as she watched her dad leave and when he closed the door behind him she asked Triangle, "Okay girl, now what really happened?"

"You know that nigga' from Flint who I be messing with?"

"Yeah, what about him? He did this to you?"

"Yes but let me tell you why!" Triangle said mysteriously as if there was a justifiable reason to beat a woman down like this.

"There ain't no reason why he should beat you like this Triangle. This is the third time he done kicked yo' ass like this! What are you gonna do with this fool? Lock him up Triangle, before he kills you," Sincere pleaded with her.

"I ain't no snitch. I ain't snitching on nobody!"

"You stupid and you sound even dumber," Sincere told her, not sparing her feelings a bit

"Well what would you do?"

CHAPTER 7

"I would tell my dad and he would take care of him quick, fast and in a hurry!" Sincere said, proud of her dad's reputation.

"Would he do it for me?"

"Umm. I don't know. If you woulda' told him the truth when you first walked in, he probably would have. Why did you lie?" Sincere asked, as she wiped some blood off her face, stopping when Triangle winced in pain.

"Because something else happened," Triangle said, as tears slowly made their way down her swollen cheek bones.

"What?" Sincere asked, wiping her tears with care.

"I saw him kill three dudes right in front of me!" Triangle said, dropping the bomb shell and releasing a heavy burden from her shoulders of keeping it a secret.

"What?" Sincere said, with shock written all over her face. "And he let you leave?"

"He said if I say anything, he would kill me too!" Triangle said, looking towards the window as if Ant was right there waiting to gun her down.

Sincere shook her head in disbelief, "So what are you gonna do Triangle? This is crazy!"

"I don't know, but I know I'm not going back to Flint!"

"How did you get here? A cab?" Sincere asked her, thinking her dad would have to give her a ride when he got home.

"His van!"

"His van? He still let you take his van?" Sincere asked her, in surprise.

"Yeah, why wouldn't he? He obviously trusts me," Triangle said, feeling a little more confident that Ant did trust her.

"So you not giving his van back?"

"No."

"Oh my god, Triangle this is ridiculous… You hungry?" Sincere asked, as she passed a burgundy towel over to her that was slightly damp.

"Naw, I ain't hungry," Triangle stated, taking the towel and gently dabbing her lip, which was still bleeding.

"Well I am, take me to get something to eat please, I'll give you gas money."

"You don't have to give me gas money, Ant gave me $300," Triangle said, pulling out wads of cash from her pockets.

They both walked outside and to the van. The tan and brown van was small, with no windows besides at the front and the rust showed along the wheel wells and in bigger pockets along the panel sides. On a day like today, with temperatures near 80 degrees out and the sun beaming down, the van looked ancient and unlikely to run. Not Sincere's choice of ride, but it was a ride.

"Phewww!" Was the first thing Sincere said as she got in on the passenger side. "It stinks in here girl!"

Triangle giggled through a swollen face and said, "It always stank in here, this is a work van girl."

"Well let's hurry up before I throw up in this work van!"

Triangle drove her to a Coney Island and had chili cheese fries to snack on while they cruised around for a bit. On their way back to Sincere's, a Pontiac police car pulled up behind them and lit them up with his flashing lights and siren.

"Shit, it's the police! I don't have my license or insurance," Triangle said nervously and thinking at worse they might have to call Sincere's dad to give them a ride.

"Relax, he probably let us go. We will just tell them we was driving to get something to eat," Sincere said, calming her friend down.

The police officer walked slowly up to the driver's side where Triangle was sitting, with his hand resting on the butt of his pistol.

"License and... What happened to your face?" The officer asked with a concerned look on his face. He looked young in the police hat, like a little boy wearing his dad's uniform. The badge sparkled in the sunlight and his leather was polished up like he was fresh from the academy.

"I got jumped," Triangle answered, going back to the original lie.

"You look like you need to go to the hospital, should I call an ambulance for you?" the officer with what looked to be a fade underneath his hat asked, reaching for his radio attached to his shirt.

"No, I'm okay! Just a little sore, but thank you," Triangle said, feeling slightly touched that he cared so much.

"Okay, well why don't you have a license plate on this van?" The officer asked, letting them know why he pulled her over.

"A..a license plate?" Triangle asked sounding like a dumb girl who didn't know shit about cars.

"Hi officer Clench. How you doing?" Sincere butted in.

"Who is that, Sincere, is that you?" He asked, with a smile, looking past Triangle.

CHAPTER 8

"Yes, this is Sincere!" she answered, bending forward so he could see her face.

"What's happening? Your daddy know you riding around in a van with no license plate on it?"

"No, he don't and neither do we or we never would've drove it."

"Well you better get on home before he does. If you get stopped again before then just tell them Officer Clench let you off with a warning and they can call me if they have a problem with that," the officer said, letting them off the hook.

"Okay, thank you and sorry about that," Sincere added with a sweet and innocent smile.

"You're welcome. Tell your dad to come down to the Den later on, okay? We'll be down there betting on the basketball game."

"Ok, I will."

"And you… get this thing off the road or get a license plate," he said, not being as nice to Triangle and sounding more official.

"It must of fell off or something," Triangle offered a feeble excuse.

"Well you better go find it before you lose this van," Clench said, doubting her story, but he wouldn't make a big deal about it with Sincere in the van.

"Okay, I will!" Triangle promised.

"Bye Officer Clench," Sincere said, as she waved at him out the window.

"Bye baby," he said as he walked back to his patrol car.

"Damn that was close girl!" Triangle said, glad Sincere was there with her.

"Yeah, you lucky I knew his ass or he would have impounded this piece of shit."

"Fuck, I gotta get a fucking plate! Ant stupid ass must have taken it off."

"And you drove all the way from Flint like that? Girl he don't give a damn about you!" Sincere said, ready to go whoop Ant's ass too.

Triangle just ignored her and pulled off going back towards Sincere's house. Later that day, they both went walking to an apartment complex that was a few minutes from Sincere's house. It didn't take them long to find a van that looked even more broke down than hers, they took the license plate off and headed back. It was getting late and Sincere knew her daddy probably wouldn't let Triangle stay the night so she had to help her get a plate in order for her to get to where she wanted to go.

"So where you staying at tonight?" Sincere asked her, worried that she would stay in the van.

"I'm going to go over to Brisco's house," Triangle said, after thinking about it for a minute. Brisco was a major drug dealer in Pontiac who was crazy about Triangle. He always looked out for her, but he also beat her up when she pissed him off.

"Okay, call me tomorrow after 6:00, I have to go to school," Sincere said, walking her to the front door.

"Okay I will," Triangle promised after hugging her friend and limping out to the van. That walk to the apartment complex had made her ankle swollen again.

Triangle had a lot of love for Sincere. Sincere was a mixed breed of black and white. Every guy wanted her, but she wasn't falling for any of their tricks, her daddy had schooled her well. Her dad also spoiled her and always let her know that she didn't need a man for nothing. All she needed to do was ask him. It didn't matter where Sincere went, guys were attracted to her, from 12 to 70 years old. Her hair was silky black and so long that it reached her ass. Sincere was a few inches taller than Triangle and her body was just as nice, if not nicer. Tight and fit, with titties so perfectly round and perky, a beautiful, angelic face and an ass that you could bounce a quarter off of.

About fifteen minutes later, Triangle pulled up to Brisco's house. He lived in an old house that was built in the early 1900's and had it renovated back to its original condition. It had five bedrooms and three baths. Brisco made it more modern with a pool and Jacuzzi out back. Triangle had just got off the phone with him, but no one answered. She wasn't going in until he came out because she couldn't stand that damn pit bull he owned. That thing was like the devil himself. She finally got out the car when he answered the phone.

CHAPTER 9

"Open the door, I'm outside," she said, feeling a little embarrassed about popping up all beat to hell, but she did warn him in advance. She needed somewhere to lay her head tonight.

"Damn, those girls wasn't playin'! They fucked you up good," Brisco said when Triangle came through the door. She was dressed in a slinky ass dress, but her face was all puffy and bruised.

Triangle giggled and said, "I guess so!" She relaxed at Brisco's house for a whole week, sunning on the pool deck. He didn't care, he loved spending time with her. He wanted her to be his girl, but she was too scared because she knew how controlling he was, and she wasn't ready to give up the freedom she craved. This was the longest she had stayed with him and they spent most of the time together having sex. Brisco was 37 years old, old enough to be her father, but Triangle didn't care. Every dude she messed with was older than she was.

After a week, Triangle begin to heal, her ribs still hurt a little and if she stepped too fast her ankle hurt, but the puffiness and bruising was fading away. With a little make-up nobody could even tell she had been beat on. "You bring clothes with you?" Brisco asked, still getting dressed while Triangle laid in the bed tangled up in the black sheets, with purple embroidered trim along the edges. She hadn't been dressed all week, even when she sun bathed it was in the nude, but Brisco had high privacy fences up, so no one could see in.

"No I didn't bring any," she admitted, thinking she was gonna have to wash the clothes she came in.

"Well I'ma run out to the mall and grab you something to put on. I'll be back shortly, I'll bring you some breakfast back too. You know what you want to eat?"

"I wanna eat you," she said jokingly as she ran her pink tongue over her full, pouty lips.

"You want some more of me girl?" Brisco asked incredulously. She was insatiable no matter how many times he laid his dick in her.

"Yep, come here!" She purred, sitting up on the bed and pulling the sheets off her body. "Take those pants off for a second and I'll show you how much I want you." She began unbuttoning his alligator belt and Armani slacks, pulling them down as she freed his hard dick from the boxers he had on.

"Yeah… Suck that dick baby," Brisco whispered while Triangle stroked him with one hand, sucking him nice and gently, just how he liked it.

"Can you fuck me before you leave?" Triangle asked, wanting to get her orgasm on too.

"Just keep sucking!" he said, grabbing the back of her head and shoving his whole dick in her hot, greedy mouth. Brisco wasn't that big in size, so she had no problem putting the thing in her mouth and keeping it there as long as she wanted. She had a special little trick she would do while she kept him in her mouth and he loved it when she wrapped her tongue around the head and sucked it.

"Turn around, let me hit that pussy! Is it wet?" he asked, looking at her pussy lips dangling there like pieces of fruit.

"It stay wet with you! An ocean never dries up baby," Triangle said, spinning around, then backing up to the edge of the bed.

Brisco entered her real aggressively and began stroking in and out of her at a fast pace. Triangle threw her ass back as always and moaned loudly. "Yes, Baby! Yes!" She screamed, loving the small sensation she got from the friction of his dick hitting her clitoris. She liked and preferred pain, but Brisco wasn't able to please her that way, but she was satisfied with the work he put in. "Harder!" she commanded him, ramming her ass back faster and faster.

"Shit, I'm bout to cum!" he said, gripping her thighs harder with his hands and meeting her ramming with his.

"Don't cum yet!" she pleaded with him, so close to getting her own nut. "Not yet!"

"I can't H..e..l.p it.. shit it's cumming!"

"No.. wait!" she ordered him, throwing her ass back even harder. She resembled a rubber band as she slung herself back and forth with his dick inside her. Brisco couldn't take it any longer, so he snatched his dick out and came all over her fine ass.

"Oh fuck! Shhiit!" he whispered, holding his dick in his hands while slapping it on her ass, while his juices squirted on her.

CHAPTER 10

Triangle was a little mad because she didn't get off herself, but she didn't say anything to him. She figured she could play with herself later on, so she just got up and grabbed a towel to wipe his nut off her ass and back.

"Alright girl, I'm outta here, I'll be back shortly. You not going to leave are you?"

"No, I'll be here when you get back," Triangle said, eyeing the pool behind Brisco's back.

"Okay, but if anyone comes by you don't have to answer the door just chill out."

Brisco left and Triangle went back to the bedroom and dived onto the bed naked. She got bored so she turned on the T.V. and started watching a movie. About thirty minutes into her movie she heard a knock at the door. It was Brisco's brother. Triangle thought about what Brisco said, but since this was his brother, she figured she'll let him in. She had met him only one time before when she was over.

"Who is it?" she asked.

"James!" he replied, and she let him in. "Where Brisco at?" he asked but already knowing. He had just got off the phone with Brisco and they was supposed to meet at the mall. Brisco had already told him that he had company at the house and told him who it was. Back when James had first seen Triangle he had wanted to fuck her and now he was gonna try behind Brisco's back.

Triangle opened the door wrapped in a sheet. "Hey, Brisco's not here right now, he'll be back shortly though."

"Oh, ok, how are you doing?" he said, walking inside.

"I'm fine… you can wait in the living room for him."

"Where you going? You aint gonna keep me company?"

"What? You want me to sit in the living room with you?" she asked, smiling.

James eye balled her trying to see through the sheet she had wrapped around her. "Yea why not?"

"Ok well let me put on some clothes real quick," Triangle said.

"Naw you straight stay like that," James said smiling. "What yall just got done fucking or something?"

"Nooo! Why?" she asked, now mad at herself for letting him in.

"You know I got a bigger dick then he does right?"

Triangle just stared, she didn't know what to say. "How would I know that, and why would I care?"

James laughed, "I just thought you should know, just in case you wanted something better and bigger."

"No I'm satisfied with what I got... Can you please leave and come back when Brisco gets here?"

"I ain't leaving, this my brother house."

"Well ok just wait out there," Triangle said then she slammed the bedroom door. Seconds later, James came busting in the room.

"You know you got a smart mouth to be so little right? You better watch who you talk to like that," He said while grabbing her neck and lifting her off the ground. Her sheet had fell revealing her naked body and her feet were inches off the floor. She was unable to scream, she kept fighting for air while he kept talking. "I should take this pussy," he said, relaxing his grip a little after seeing how purple she was turning. She came back to her feet and was able to breathe again.

"Please get out," she said, holding her neck trying to catch her breath.

"Give me some pussy and I'll go, no problem."

Triangle started crying. "No, I'm not!"

"You gonna do what the fuck I tell you to do. Now bend over!"

Triangle cried even harder. She was shaking and didn't know what to do and she didn't want to get beat up again or choked. She was just praying that Brisco came back and walked in. James soon took her by the wrist and forced her to turn around. She did and he pulled out his dick and began raping her. His big hard dick tore through the soft tender skin. She couldn't help but cry even more from all the pain. Her insides were not even moist, so she was able to feel every inch he forced inside of her. She wasn't able to take the pain so, she stretched out on her stomach hoping he would stop, but he straddled her booty and kept stroking her deeply and hard as he could. Tears raced down her face onto the sheets for what seemed like forever. She wanted to scream so bad because all the pain, but was just too scared. Soon she felt him shake and she felt warm lava shoot inside her up to her chest and it was over.

James pulled his pants up with a smile, "Next time have that pussy ready for me because I'm gonna take it whenever

I see you, no matter where we at. You hear me?" He got no answer. So he slapped her real hard on her booty cheek. "You hear me?"

"Y..y.yeah," she whispered, burning in pain. It felt like her pussy was on fire. She just curled up under the sheets and cried.

CHAPTER 11

James left after he got dressed, then he arrived back with his brother Brisco 4 hours later. When Brisco walked in the room, Triangle had it spotless. She had cleaned everything up, including herself and was wearing a pair of his hoop shorts, with one of his plain red t-shirts. Her pussy was still hurting, even though she soaked in steaming hot bath water. She didn't even feel comfortable sitting down.

"Whatsup, you good?" Brisco asked, setting the food and new bags on the bed. "I got you some French toast, eggs, bacon and an orange juice."

"Thank you," Triangle said, doing her best to smile.

"You remember my brother James? James this is Triangle, I think you met before, a while ago."

"Yeah, I remember her. How you doing?" James asked, giving Triangle a slick look behind Brisco's back.

"I'm fine," Triangle lied. She wanted to tell Brisco so bad, but she was scared. So scared that he might not believe her, scared that someone might hurt her again, just scared of being scared. If she did say something and Brisco did believe her, then he would be pissed off for sure at his brother. Even with what James had done to her she did not want them to get into a fight over her. She had seen too much and the memories of those dead bodies came rushing back to her like a tidal wave. Triangle got on the bed and ate while Brisco and James talked in the living room. After Triangle was done eating, she began getting dressed. Brisco had bought her two outfits, and two pair of shoes, two bra and panties set, and some hygiene items that she needed. Brisco wanted to take care of Triangle and a small part of her longed for that, but now the small amount of safety she had felt was shattered. That could not be undone and no amount of clothes or gifts could make up for that. Plus, Triangle was tied to too many people and she didn't know how to break away even if she wanted to. Soon as she finished getting dressed she was heading for the door.

"Bye Brisco, I'll call you soon," she said.

"You leaving me already baby?"

"You not tired of me yet?" she asked, with a smile trying her hardest to avoid looking at James who was sitting right on the couch next to Brisco.

"I ain't never tired of you girl… Where you going?"

"To visit my grandmother," she lied, while trying to figure out the real answer to that question herself.

"Well here, put this in your pocket," he said, peeling off three $50 bills and handing it to her.

"Thank you," she said, leaving out the door. She hadn't been in the van for a whole week, all she kept doing was praying that it started up and she was able to get away from James, far away. Soon as she got in the van the smell was overwhelming. It was the worst smell she had ever smelled in her life.

"Damn! Sincere is right, this van does smell horrible," she said out loud as she put the key in the ignition and prayed it would start. Thankfully it started and she quickly put the windows down and drove straight to Sincere's house. The bodies in the back were starting to smell stronger and stronger and she had no idea that they were there. The shock of all that had happened to her was starting to take a toll. Had she walked around the back of the van she would have seen the blood leaking slowly out under the van doors onto the street. When she was about three minutes away from Sincere's house, she picked up her cell phone and called her.

"Hello," Sincere answered.

"Girl I've been calling you all morning!"

"I told you I had school today. Girl I'm at school right now!"

"Oh shit, I didn't know, I drove all the way over to your house for nothing then. I had wanted you to ride to Detroit with me. I'm about to go see my white boyfriend. He gonna be mad at me though because I haven't been answering my phone."

"Who you talking about, David?" Sincere asked, having a hard time keeping track of all the guys she be with.

"Yeah, who else? You know I don't mess with many white boys like that."

"Whatever… you mess with whoever," Sincere said, as a joke, but meaning it.

"You just about to pop up over there?"

"Girl I have a key to his condo," Triangle bragged about her mad skills at reeling in men. "I can go whenever I want!"

"Why don't you just go stay over there and get your life together? You can't just look good forever!" Sincere said, picturing her friend walking the streets twenty years from now to make money.

"Girl, I'm not about to go stay with none of these dudes. All they want to do is put their hands on me, so that's why I bounce around like I do. I'ma pimp."

"Girl you crazy! If you so pimp, why you riding around in that stankin' ass van?"

"Now you know why I got the windows down instead of the A/C on. It don't smell so bad now!" Triangle said, still feeling like her stomach was a little upset from the smell or the past few days.

"You need to tell David to let you drive one of his cars and park that ugly ass van!"

Triangle giggled at the way Sincere was all whispering right in the middle of class. "This van is low key girl, but okay, I'ma get one of David's cars and come get you from school, what time you get out?"

"Naw, I'll just call you when I get home!"

"Okay, talk to you later!" Triangle hung up and headed for I-75, a straight shot to Detroit and David's house.

David was a white guy, who was an accountant for rich people. He was older, 39 years old with kids he didn't have custody of. He was always lonely, so he paid prostitutes on a daily basis, but as with most men, he was in love with Triangle. He had met her in Southfield, on the side of a road with a flat tire. He helped her change it and they exchanged phone numbers. She went over to his house a few times after that and let him eat her pussy, then they eventually started having sex. He liked Triangle a lot, but he hated it when she would leave for weeks at a time with no word from her.

CHAPTER 12

When Triangle was close to David's house she called his number.

"Hello, David speaking," the self-confident business voice said on the other end.

"Hey David," she purred into the phone.

"Hi! Is this Triangle?" he asked, hoping it was, he was itching to finally crack that pussy open.

"Yes, it is! How are you baby?" she asked, sounding sexy with no effort.

"I'm fine, how are you? Hold on a second," he said having to turn his phone up a little louder. "Okay, I was barely able to hear you. You calling from a wind tunnel or something? Never mind that, the real question is, when am I going to be able to see you?"

Giggling, Triangle answered sweet as silk, "Right now if you want. I just pulled up in front of your place."

"You did? Say you swear!" David replied, unable to hide or contain his excitement. "Well what are you waiting for? Come in goof ball!"

Triangle laughed this time, "Okay, give me a second, I have to park this raggedy ass van some place!"

"Shoot, just put it in my garage, there's an open spot in there," he offered as he pressed a button on his cell phone to make the garage door open.

"Then I guess I'll be there in a minute," she said driving into the garage. She was so happy to get out of the stinking van. She figured it was either some spoiled food or she ran over an animal and its guts and carcass were sizzling into the tires. She quickly grabbed her purse, almost having to hold her breath and a few other bags off the passenger seat and went inside.

Every piece of furniture David owned was black and white, same kind of white, retro style she guessed. Each time she came over his place was immaculate, like OCD spotless. Whoever cleaned this place had to be exhausted trying to please him.

Going from the putrid, smelling van to this house was a welcome relief to her. David had a big goofy grin on his face when Triangle walked through the attached garage door. "Hi sweetie!" he said with his hands open for a hug. David enveloped her in his arms and then grabbed her bags from her. "So how long do I get to have the pleasure of your company this time?" he asked her, hoping it was longer. David was a pudgy, pasty skinned, white boy. He never worked out and you could see indulgences of good wine and food in his ever expanding waist line. His receiving hair line was winning the fight over his head, and his cheeks were bulging out like a chipmunk with food in its mouth. His wardrobe was the basic yuppie suits or sports coat with dress shirt, but overall, David was a sweet and giving man. His ex-wife was a bitch who dogged his ass every chance she got, and used his kids as ammunition to get more money from him.

Triangle smiled like a sex kitten and replied, "I don't know! David! We'll have to see how bad I'm wanted!"

"Oh you're wanted! I told you to come move in with me, I'll take good care of you baby doll!"

"I don't know about that David, but I'm here now!"

Not wanting to push things and make her leave he said, "Okay, make yourself at home, anything you need, just ask!" Even though he offered anything, he also knew Triangle well enough to know she wouldn't really be asking for anything, and even if she did, it would be something small. He had plenty of money and he was more than willing to spend it on Triangle. He regularly embezzled money from his clients and spent his time washing it into overseas accounts and then when it came out clean on the other side, he invested it. Over the years, it had earned him a sizeable amount of untraceable money.

CHAPTER 13

"Well, right now I need a vehicle to drive. You think you could help me with that?" Triangle asked, bending over to let him look down her shirt.

"For sure! I have a couple cars I hardly ever drive, it will be good to get them out and put some mileage on them. Of course, I can't let you drive the Porsche because it's a stick shift, which you don't know how to drive. How does a four door Infiniti sound to you?"

"That's fine, anything besides that gross van I've been driving around in," Triangle said, sounding truly excited and grateful without even knowing what an Infiniti was.

"You know I don't mind, you can take it whenever. Here are the keys!" he said, handing them to her with a gas card attached to it so she would never have to worry about money to fill it up. "Just make sure you don't leave me again for longer than two days," he commented with a big dopey smile on his face.

"Thank you," Triangle replied, returning a smile and adding a wink. They stayed in for the rest of the day, while

David talked and bored her to death about the stock market and his investments. She made a mental note to call Sincere in the morning. Triangle was dreading tonight because her pussy was still sore from when James raped her. Even sitting still for too long was uncomfortable. She definitely didn't want to have sex, even to let him lick her pussy, which usually made her happy, was the opposite tonight. She could see it in David's eyes that he wanted to have sex. His dick was bulging beneath his perfectly creased, tailored pants. He made his usual, predictable move of putting his hand on her thigh, waiting for permission instead of being aggressive. Not meaning to, she recoiled from his touch, which made him pursue her like she was playing hard to get. She was too embarrassed to tell him what happened.

"Come on Triangle, you know I want you. It has been too long already," he said inching closer. Although he was just with a prostitute last night, she was not even as good looking as Triangle was.

"I don't want to have sex right now, but I do enjoy laying here with you," Triangle said hoping he was cool with that.

"Well at least let me finger you or something?" David asked, lying next to her, rubbing his hardness against her, after pulling his shirt off and unveiling his sagging love handles and almost the same size breast that Triangle had.

"No David, don't you get it? I don't want anything in my pussy right now! Can I just rest, please?" Triangle pleaded with him.

"No I want to fuck you right now, quit playing with me!"

"I'm not playing with you, I don't feel like fucking right now," Triangle said, pushing him away from her and trying to get out of the bed.

"That's bullshit Triangle and you know it! Come over here and tease me like this!" he said angrily, as he got out of the bed really aggressively. Triangle laid back down when he got up, wondering why guys wanted to have sex with her instead of just being there for her in other ways. Then she felt a tug on her legs, it was David yanking her to the floor.

"Whaat…The…Fuck…You…doing..? Stop!" she screamed as she fell to a heap beneath his sweating, layers of fat.

"You leave me for days, fucking all those black guys, but you bring your shit to my house? Spend the night and have the nerve to say I can't have sex with you? I want you out of here, right now!" he shouted. "I'm sick of your shit!"

"Stop!" she screamed as he got off of her and began dragging her down the hall while she tried to grab ahold of furniture, doors, anything to stop the carpet burn that felt like it was skinning her flesh off. "Okay! You can fuck me! Please stop David!"

"So this is what it takes I see!" he yelled as he stop dragging her. "Is this what I have to do to get you to fuck me?"

"What?" she asked, trying not to cry.

"I have to put my hands on you, right?"

"No you don't have to do this David," Triangle begged, as she shook her head at him.

"Yes I do!" David said like a crazy man, as he picked her up off the floor by her hair. "Yeah, you like to be beat don't you?" he shouted, as he directed her by the hair back to the bathroom.

Trying to walk so he didn't rip her hair off, she screamed, "No! Please let my hair go!" she didn't want to fight back because she was scared, so she just let him take advantage of her. He stripped off the little night gown she was wearing and ripped the panties off her hips, like they were made of paper.

"This is how you like it?" he asked, while he climbed on top of her and began thrusting his dick inside her. All she could do was lay there and cry. He was tearing her skin where it had started to heal, re damaging the tissue inside of her.

"Ow! Ouch! Please stop!" she begged, trying to get away from him and the pain.

"Shut up and take it! Just take it! You like that don't you?" he asked still pumping her full of meat, going as hard as he could, slamming his pelvic bone into hers.

His crushing weight and the pain from inside was suffocating her, to the point where she thought she was gonna pass out.

"Ouch! Please stop David!" she sobbed after each hard, deep stroke into her swollen pussy. "Fuck! Fuck! That hurts!" she cried out in vain. All she felt was more and more pain, which seemed to only increase his pleasure. Her pussy wasn't wet, yet he kept jamming his dick inside with no apparent sympathy. He was blinded by his sexual rage. Finally he pulled his dick out and Triangle saw blood on the head of it, moments before a big squirt of nut flew straight into her face, covering her eyes and nose.

"Ahaa yeah! Baby, yeah!" he moaned while jerking himself off and squirting more of his fluids on her face. He got off of her and waddled into the bathroom to clean himself up. "You could have told me you was on your period!" he yelled from the bathroom, but Triangle had no words. She just laid there with tears streaming down her face and blood leaking from her bruised and battered pussy. She knew she wasn't on her period. The friction from his dick had made her skin raw inside. The fire inside was the worst feeling she could imagine. It felt like her pussy was engulfed in flames and there was no amount of water to put it out. She got up and tried to wipe herself off with some toilet paper. Every time she touched it, her red and sensitive pussy stung. She was in so much pain, three different ways of killing herself flashed through her brain: The first way was shooting herself, but after seeing those three men shot, that did not sit well with her. Then she thought about hanging herself, but she figured that would hurt even more.

Her last idea was to drown herself, but she decided on a hot bath instead, since inhaling water was also painful. Sitting in the tub, as the jet streams pulsated against her sore body, she tried to go over the events from the last couple of weeks. It seemed like all the men in her life hurt her instead of loving her. She was tired of getting raped. She was tired of them using her as a sex object. She cried, adding more water to the tub and prayed for God to take the burden of what felt like the whole world, off her back. A burden she was not strong enough to carry on her own. What she really wanted was a man to return the love she felt, without any pain involved. She soaked in the bath for almost an hour. David's tub was huge, big enough for three people, and his condo was enormous, but to Triangle that just made it feel even emptier.

CHAPTER 14

Triangle stepped out of the tub and stopped to look at herself in the full length mirror. Her face was puffy from crying. She could see the pain and loneliness in her eyes and it seemed like the harder she tried to fill the void in her heart, men just filled the void in her pussy or other painful ways. She shaved her legs and pussy area clean and then returned to the bedroom, so exhausted. David was already fast asleep and snoring on the bed. A part of her wanted to kill him right there, but a bigger part of her was tired of the killing and all the pain. Tired of feeling lonely, abandoned and hurt, she climbed into the bed with him and snuggled up against his sleeping body. She freely chose the option of getting into the bed and sleeping next to him. Even as tired as she was, she laid there, trying not to move for a couple of hours. The pain was so intense, she finally decided to get up and found some petroleum jelly to rub on and inside of her pussy to quell the pain. Feeling a little better, she was able to slide into the bed next to him and drift off to sleep with a million thoughts racing through her mind.

The next morning Triangle woke up with David's dick inside of her. "Yeah, you're nice and wet this morning baby!" David said, humping away on her. "Your pussy feels so good!" Triangle was in pain again, but this time at least it didn't hurt as much because of the petroleum jelly she had rubbed on there. She actually felt a little sensation down there, the begging of an orgasm, but perhaps that feeling was because she was able to lay next to David all night holding him. A part of her wanted to make him happy because of that, even if that meant enduring a little pain. She still felt the burn, but now it was a small flame, not a raging inferno. It felt like a piece of her was missing inside. Really this was a feeling she was used to since she always seemed to feel like a piece of her heart was missing too.

"Please go slow David," she whispered. She tried to hide the tears running down her face, but still couldn't help but to arch her back off the bed with her head titled back.

"Ahh!.. Ouch! Slow Down!" she pleaded with him, but David was lost in his own little world of her pussy. He sped up, going faster and faster, until he snatched his dick out of her and came on her face again. This time she tried to dodge the nut as it splashed out, but he grabbed her hair.

When he was done, he got off her and went to get ready for work.

"Triangle, you got some good pussy!" he yelled from the bathroom.

"Thanks," she said sarcastically, not really knowing what else to say.

"I'm going to be leaving soon. If you leave be sure to set the alarm on the house and if you take the car, be back by midnight," he said, kissing her on the cheek and leaving for the day.

"Okay," she responded. She couldn't wait to get away from him and the house of pain it represented. She picked up her phone and called Sincere crying.

"Hello! Girl, what happened to you yesterday? You never called!"

"S..o.orr.y," Triangle said, sniffling into the phone as she fought her tears back.

"What's wrong?" Sincere asked, dreading whatever drama her friend found herself in now.

"David… he raped me last night and again this morning!"

CHAPTER 15

"He raped you?" Sincere asked, wondering why he would do that when her friend gave that shit away like government cheese.

"Y..e..ah," Triangle said, sobbing away to her friend.

"Where are you?" Sincere asked with worry in her voice.

"Still at his house," Triangle said, realizing how odd that sounded.

"He won't let you leave? You want me to call the police? Do you have transportation?"

"No, I can leave and he let me use his car."

"So let me get this straight, he rapes you and then let you use his car?" Sincere asked, thinking her friend was on drugs.

"Yeah!" Triangle said. She knew how stupid she sounded, even to herself.

Sincere didn't know what to think about Triangle sometimes. Her life seemed so strange like every time she called, something new and bad had happened, and yet Triangle always came out fairly okay. She was a survivor and no one could dispute that, but she was afraid that one of these days her luck was gonna run out and she'd read or hear about her friend being killed and dumped in some abandoned house or dumpster.

Back pedaling a little Triangle said, "Well he didn't rape me rape me, but I didn't want to have sex with him and he forced me to."

"Well that sounds like rape to me! I don't get it," Sincere said, sounding confused.

"Never mind Sincere, I need to go to the hospital. My pussy is still on fire!"

"You want me to go with you?" Sincere asked sounding more concerned now and doubting her less.

"Yes please, I don't want to go alone!"

"Okay, come get me! I'm at home!"

"Okay, I'ma get in the shower and get dressed and I'll be there soon girl," Triangle promised as she hung up the phone.

Triangle went into the bathroom and took another long bath then got dressed. Before she left out the door, she noticed an envelope on the door with her name written on it. She opened the envelope and it had a small note inside that read, "Go buy yourself something nice." It also had $400 inside. She smiled to herself and skipped out the door feeling special and appreciated. She got into the red, with black trim Infiniti and it took her almost five minutes to figure out how to start it. One thing she knew, she did not miss the horrible smelling van. This car was brand new, the mileage read, "000798". *Not even a thousand miles yet*, she thought to herself as she worked the power seats and mirrors, feeling like a pilot of a space shuttle. This was the nicest car that Triangle had ever drove and she wasn't really looking forward to going to the hospital, but she knew she needed to get checked out. Something was definitely wrong down there. Her pussy was still on fire and it hurt to sit in the car, so she drove as fast as she could to Sincere's house.

"Hey girl!" Sincere said, smiling as she got in the car. "Girl, this David's Infiniti?"

"Yeah, why you like it?" Triangle asked, already knowing the answer by the look of awe on Sincere's face.

"Hell yeah! I love these cars! You got it made, where you be finding all these dudes at?"

"Girl, you know I be everywhere!"

Sincere laughed, "And you looking cute as hell with your face all healed up!"

"Thank you!" Triangle said, driving to keep her eyes on the road and not think about where they were driving to. She parked and went straight into the E.R. Three long hours later, Triangle found out she had a severe bacterial infection. They gave her some ointment and antibiotic's to take for ten days. They also advised her not to have sex for ten days either, because her insides were very swollen. Leaving the hospital, they stopped at a pharmacy and then drove to Pontiac. Brisco was calling Triangle back to back and texting her.

"Why don't you answer the phone?" Sincere asked her, surprised a little.

"All he wanna do is fuck!" Triangle said, not wanting to tell her the real reason, that she was afraid of James finding out she was there.

"Ohh, when you go back to school? How long you get kicked out for?" Sincere asked, not paying attention to the quiver in her voice when Triangle thought of James.

"Three weeks!" she replied back, trying to get James out of her head.

"Girl, you gotta get it together. You supposed to be in college with me," Sincere said, reminding her of the plan they made a few years ago.

"I know, I know. I will soon, I promise!" Triangle replied, looking happier now that Sincere was still in her corner.

CHAPTER 16

"When are you going back to your grandma's house? You know she needs you over there to help her with things. She been calling over my place and my dad's cell phone everyday looking for you. That's part of the reason my dad don't like you over there, he don't need you to be reported as a runaway and have the police all over there in his business!"

"My grandma is crazy. She thinks I drink, smoke weed and fuck!" Triangle complained to Sincere. "Oh and of course, fight in school too."

"Well she almost got it all right. You do be fighting girls. You need to use some of those techniques on them dudes that be beating on you all the time!"

Triangle giggled, at the thought of beating them up, like Halle Berry in "Cat Woman". "Those dudes are strong, now I can wrestle a little bit with Lamar, but that's about it."

"You still be messin' with Lamar?"

"Yeah, I was just on the phone with him, but I ain't seen him in a couple of weeks," Triangle said, amazed in her mind about all the men that have been in and out of her life.

"So when are you going home?" Sincere asked, bringing the conversation back to that, a subject Triangle hated, and did not want to talk about. She loved the freedom of going anywhere she wanted.

"I don't know Sincere, soon!" Triangle said, tired of riding her head about it all the time. They cruised all over Pontiac then stopped at a gas station to fill up and get some snacks on David's gas card. Then they headed to Detroit and rode around longer than they intended. They made what was supposed to be a quick stop at the mall a mini shopping spree. By the time they got done and came out, it was 9:00 p.m. Triangle called Ant like ten times in the mall, but didn't get an answer. *He must be with a bitch,* she thought to herself. "Can you ride with me somewhere real quick before I take you home?"

"Yeah, where we going?" Sincere asked, knowing her dad would be mad because she was supposed to be home doing her homework, but she thought maybe he wouldn't be in until later.

"To Flint for a minute," she replied, driving all the way to Flint as the setting sun winked in the west. It was close to 11:00 p.m. by the time they arrived there because of an accident. Triangle didn't park in front of Ant's house. She instead chose a parking spot a couple of houses away. "Girl I'll be right back!"

"Where you going with a screwdriver? I know you aint stalkin' this crazy nigga? Didn't you just see him kill three people?" Sincere asked her, as the door shut out anymore words from her. Sincere was pissed now that Triangle just brought her to the scene of a triple murder.

Triangle disregarded her friend's questions and crept up to the house and began looking in the windows. Sincere awaited in the car for almost an hour waiting for Triangle to return. She was beginning to get nervous, so she jumped over to the driver's side and she figured she would wait a little longer before she went looking for her friend. Looking out the window, she was startled by the sound of two shots ringing out into the night. She looked where the flashes came from. Then she saw the bright colors of Triangle's clothes running towards her. Sincere started up the car and unlocked the doors. Gun shots rang out again, with two of them finding the rear windows of the Infiniti. One whizzed past Sincere face as she screamed, ducking down to avoid any more incoming rounds. The passenger door opened and Triangle jumped in, "Go! Go!" Triangle yelled, panicked and scared.

Bullets careened off and into the car as they drove off, both in fear of their lives. In the process of leaving, Sincere scraped the side of the vehicle they were parked next to, spraying sparks as the two metal met. Turning the first corner, the car railed on two wheels before setting back down, and they no longer heard any shots.

"What the fuck was that?" Sincere asked, her voice trembling and her hands shaking as she tried to steer straight.

Triangle was silent for a second and then said, "That nigga' just crazy! We straight girl, don't worry!" Triangle tried to reassure her friend although she didn't think they were straight at all.

"Fuck that! I ain't fucking wit' you no more! You trying to get me killed!" Sincere said, heading home, not caring if she was hurting her friend feelings or not.

"We good girl, chill out!"

"Naw, we not good at all, we coulda got killed!" Sincere said, pissed at Triangle and all the dudes she be fucking with. She didn't say another word to Triangle and when she got home, she got out and went inside, leaving Triangle feeling even lonelier than ever.

CHAPTER 17

Triangle was scared to drive David's car back to him with it all shot up, so instead she did what all people do when they feel lonely and have nowhere to go, she went home.

Her grandmother was sleeping when she got there, so she parked the car in the back so a passing squad car wouldn't see it and she fell to sleep. Early the next morning, Triangle's grandmother noticed that she had come back. Triangle's grandma was young to be a grandma at 55, but she had her daughter young, just as Triangle's mother had her young. She wanted to help Triangle get back on track so she wouldn't ruin her life, but she didn't know how, so she did the only thing she could think of, she called her Uncle Phillip.

Phillip was sitting on his cream colored, leather sofa, wearing some black hoop shorts, socks and a white T-shirt as he watched a reality show on his fifty-inch plasma that hung on the wall. He let his phone ring a few times and finally answered it when he figured they weren't going to give up.

"Hello!" Philip said, perhaps a little too roughly when he found out it was his mom on the phone.

"Hey, how are you? Did I call you at a bad time?" she asked, noticing the way he answered.

"I'm good mom, I was just watching some TV. How are you?" he asked, not trying to get into a fight with her. He knew he would pay for it down the road.

"Not so good actually! This girl is driving me crazy, she don't do nothing but fight in school, drink, smoke, probably fuck and suck, and God knows what else," she said, unleashing all her frustrations to her son, not caring about her vulgar language.

"Who are you talking about Ma? Not Triangle I hope?" Phillip asked, a little confused as he tried to look at what was happening on TV as well.

"Of course I'm talking about Triangle, your damn niece has gone crazy and she is trying her best to take me with her or end up like her mother! I just don't know what else to do. I wish her mother or father was here, maybe they could get through to her."

"Yeah, that might help if they were able to give good advice," he said, knowing that was really not a possibility.

"Well, what should I do? Your girls are in college and prolly will be done with that soon. What the hell did you do to get them right? Raising boys seems a little easier. I'm not sure what to do," she confessed, almost at the end of her rope.

"Well I can't promise you anything, but I'll tell you what. Why don't you bring her by this weekend and let me talk to her?"

"I don't know if she'll stay that long, I can bring her over now. She's kicked out of school for fighting."

"Oh, well bring her by then. Tell her to just pack her underwear and other things, no clothes though. That should make her want to come if she thinks there's shopping involved," Phillip said, thinking of what he could do to make a difference in her life.

His mom laughed, "You got that right! You got me wanting to pack my stuff and come with her."

Phillip laughed too, "You can come over whenever you want ma. I'll be here waiting."

"Okay, give me an hour and I'll be there to drop her off. Thanks Phillip, I love you. Thanks for trying to help."

"All right ma, I love you too and that's what family are for," Phillip said, hanging up as the end of his show was going off. Good thing he had the DVR going.

After Phillip hung up the phone, he looked to see what he was wearing and then went to change. He knew he had to dress a little younger so his niece would think he was hip and maybe listen to his advice. He saw what was happening to little boys and girls in the world today. The boys were all interested in bling and big rims, the girls were chasing the boys that they felt had the money, was the shit or had all the girls. Then the boys was chasing money, selling drugs, robbing, or whatever else to keep their fronts up, making the girls think they had it like that.

Phillip put on a yellow, white and navy blue, plaid button up, with navy blue denim shorts, white shoes and fitted cap to match. He even put on his gold jewelry consisting of a pinky ring that was three carats. A lengthy gold chain with an iced out charm that was seven carats, and an expensive black band watch with a gold, ten carat diamond face. When he was satisfied with his appearance, he called his friend and they traded cars for a few days. Phillip switched his yellow mustang for his friend's Cadillac pick-up truck, which was all white, with matching 26 inch rims. Phillip knew he was going pretty far, but was willing to do anything to save his niece's life. He didn't want to hear rumors down the road of her prostituting and fucking everybody in the hood for sneakers, weed or hair-dos. Nor did he want to one day see her on the pole of some cracked out strip club. He had already raised his two girls, 19 and 20 year old respected and classy women, and far from being conceited or petty. They were both down to earth and they would help anyone that needed it, not because they were getting anything out of it, but because it was the right thing to do. They were hard workers, no matter how menial the job was. The two of them had been the prettiest girls in high school and worked at a burger joint, slinging burgers for minimum wage, and didn't care what anybody thought. They always kept in mind what their dad told them, *"People hate on you no matter if you're doing good or bad."* They both believed that and they saw that it was true as they got older. Today, with the burger joint far behind them, they worked their butts off at a law firm and people still talk bad about them, being stuck up and whatever else negative they could possibly think of.

CHAPTER 18

Phillip heard a knock at the door and knew it had to be his mom dropping off Triangle, but he looked out the peep hole just to be sure and saw one person standing on his porch, *Triangle.*

He opened the door with a smile and welcomed her, "Hey baby girl!" He waved her inside and gave her a big hug. She was carrying a small book bag, made by a popular designer, wearing a pair of stretch Capri pants, a purple short sleeve button up shirt that stopped right on top of her round booty. She was also wearing purple heels that matched her outfit.

"Hey!" she said, smiling back, looking so innocent.

"Wow, you're beautiful! It's been a long time since I've seen you. You sure have grown up, look at you now, looking like a woman! How old are you?"

"Seventeen, my birthday was last month," she said proudly.

"Oh, okay, I missed that... Did you have a party?" he asked, taking her bag and waving goodbye to his mom in the driveway. He closed the door and turned towards Triangle and the mission at hand.

"Naw, for my birthday I just went to the club, out to eat and the movies… oh and shopping, which is all my favorite things to do. Whose truck is that outside Uncle Phil?"

"That's my home boy's truck, I was borrowing it to see if I could get some girls while driving it. What you think? You think I can pull in some girls with that?"

Triangle smiled again, "I know you'll get some girls in that! That boy on fleek!"

"That boy on fleek? What that mean?" he asked her, looking really confused and out of his league.

Triangle giggled at her uncle, "That means the car is fresh, or it's cute, you know?"

"Oh, okay! I'm old school. I don't know a lot of new slang… Well let's get out of here and hit a couple of stores."

"Cool, can I drive?" she asked, looking at him with her big, puppy dog eyes.

"You got license?"

"No, not yet, but I'll have it next month. I got a permit though, as long as you have a license I can drive," she told him, hoping she could get behind the wheel.

"Na, if it was mine I would let you. I wanna talk to you about some things anyway. All I want you to do is sit back, listen and ride."

"Okay!" she said, a little disappointed at not getting to drive. She had no clue on what he wanted to talk about. She didn't know that her grandma had told him all the bad stuff she had been doing. She just thought her uncle wanted to spend some time with her and take her shopping because his girls were all grown up. They both got in the truck and left, as the radio played on low volume.

"So what's going on with you? How are your grades in school?" he asked, starting with small stuff and working his way to the more serious.

"I'm okay! They're okay."

"They okay? What's okay?" he asked, joking around. "You can be honest with me. I understand what being a teenager is like, not only a teenager but a young adult, because that's what you are right now."

"Well right now I'm failing because I keep getting kicked out!"

"Kicked out for what?" he asked, even though he knew the answer.

"For fighting!"

"For what?"

"What am I fighting for?"

"Yeah!"

"Because females keep my name in they mouth! All they do is talk about me behind my back, then when I ask them they act like they don't know what I'm talking about."

Phillip laughed at her, "So you fighting because people keep talking junk about you, good or bad?"

"Yeah, but it's all bad!"

"What are they saying?"

"Stuff like I'm a hoe, I fucked the whole…oops I cursed!"

"It's okay, continue. You fucked..?"

"They just be hating!" she said not explaining who she fucked.

"Do it be true?"

"NO!" she said, crossing her arms in protest.

"Well then why do you let it bother you to the point you gotta put hands on someone?"

"Because they be lying!"

"But you know what they say isn't who you are right?"

"Yeah!"

"So why does what they say about you matter?"

"Uncle, you just don't understand, they…"

"I do understand! You don't want yourself to look bad towards anybody else. You feel like they trying to ruin your reputation right?"

"Well… Yeah kind of! I just don't like when people keep my name in they mouth, so I check them about it. What is you talking about me for, or do you just wanna get yo' ass whopped?" Triangle said real aggressively. This really surprised him.

"Listen baby girl, when people not talking about you, that's when you should be worried, but other than that, let them talk. Why let them prevent you from getting an education?"

"Oh I'm still gonna get that!" she said, so sure of herself.

"I understand that, but why let them prolong it?"

"You right, so don't fight in school?" she asked teasing him.

"Stop playing, don't fight at all unless they swing first!" he said, and they both laughed.

"I don't know, maybe I just have a bad temper!"

"That's fine baby, as long as you learn to control it instead of letting it control you. You have to find another outlet for your temper besides fighting. Some people work out, others box, martial arts," Phillip said, trying to make sense of what he was saying. Triangle nodded her head up and down, beginning to see that her uncle really seemed to know what he was talking about. "You never let someone knock you off your square, don't even let people know that they can make you mad, fly above all the haters baby, like Kandi says."

CHAPTER 19

Triangle giggled, knowing her uncle was making sense. "So if a girl hit me first I can get it on?"

"Yeah, that's when you beat her ass, then you're not the one who instigated it, but don't let words provoke you into harming another person."

"What if she call my mama a bitch?" Triangle asked, not even trying to clean up her language this time.

Phillip laughed, "Just don't fight…Do you have a job?" he asked, quickly changing the subject because he felt like he was talking in circles.

"Naw, aint nobody hiring."

"So is this why you letting them petty ass girls get to you?"

"No!"

"It's got to be. I bet if you had a job to go to or something else important, you wouldn't care what them people said. You know that's bull shit about no one is hiring, don't you? I can take you into any city and show you help wanted signs," Phillip told her, making sure she didn't get shit twisted. Triangle just sat there with a thoughtful look on her face.

"I'm gonna get you a job!" Phillip declared out of the blue.

Surprised Triangle asked, "Where?" sounding a little excited now.

"Where? What you mean where? Why does it matter where? Are you making any money now doing something legal?"

"No!" Triangle responded, wondering if he put the legal thing because he knew she was doing something.

"Well then, it shouldn't matter baby. You know Unk love you. I'ma hook you up, but you gotta get rid of that ego and chip you have going on."

"What ego?" she asked trying to act like she didn't know what he was talking about, but really knowing better. While she pondered the question, the phone rang again and she looked down to see it was David calling. She knew he was gonna be pissed about not bringing the car back, but she didn't have a clue what to tell him. How was she gonna explain getting his car shot up and wrecked? "Hello!" she answered. Triangle stayed on the phone for about five minutes before she hung up.

"Dang who was that?"

"My boyfriend," she lied.

"Your boyfriend who?"

"You want to meet him? He just asked me to bring him something to eat. Can we make that happen Unk?" she asked him, hoping he said yes.

"Where he at?" He thought maybe he could get to the bottom of her behavior if he met some of her friends, especially boyfriends.

"Can I drive when we get near his place?" Triangle asked him again, flashing her big, brown eyes at him trying to get her way.

Phillip turned to look at her and asked, "No! For what?"

"Just because," she said almost in a little girl whisper.

"Oh I see, you like impressing and showing out?"

Triangle giggled again, because he was right. "Not just that, I want him to see me pushing this big body!"

"Oh okay. What's this lil' guy want to eat?"

"Just go to the Coney Island, he likes mozzarella sticks, chili cheese fries, and a couple of foot longs," she told Phillip.

20 minutes later they pulled up in front of a house where five different cars were parked. They all had expensive, big rims on them, new and old cars.

"Right here," Triangle instructed, about to get out.

"Wait, where you going? Make him come and get it," Phillip told her. He was curious to get a good look at him.

Triangle waved her hand for him to come off the porch. Lamar walked up and smiled with two gold teeth in his mouth, no shirt on, tatted all over, hat to one side, with some blue shorts on that were saggin'. He looked like he could be the rapper Plies little brother.

"What's up?" Phillip asked, leaning past Triangle and put his hand out for Lamar to shake.

"What's up? How you doing?" Lamar asked, shaking his hand pretty firmly.

"I'm good, how about yourself?"

"I'm straight," he responded as he grabbed the bags of food. "Thanks boo!"

"Thanks? Where the money at for that?" Phillip asked, stopping Lamar in his tracks.

Lamar laughed, "Oh, it ain't nothing. I got that," he replied smugly, as he dug into his pocket and pulled out a dealer's wad of cash. He peeled a ten off and handed it to her. Triangle face turned red when her uncle asked him to pay for it.

"So this is your little girlfriend right here?"

"Yeah," he answered going along with the text message that Triangle had sent before getting there.

"You know this my niece right?"

"Yeah, I do now!" Lamar answered in a way that told Phillip he wanted to get away from there in a hurry.

"You used to women paying for your food?" Phillip asked him, not liking his kind at all.

Triangle turned and looked at him with her eyes wide as a watermelon. "Please uncle, don't!" she whispered out of the side of her mouth. Phillip saw he was embarrassing her and stopped talking.

"Don't mind him Lamar. He's a little over protective. I'll talk to you later okay."

"Okay baby!" Lamar replied, and as he went to walk away, out of nowhere black cars pulled in from every direction. A helicopter hovered overhead and you could hear voices yelling, "Police! Freeze!" as canine units pulled up with German Shepherds lunging at the window to be released. That was all they heard before being ordered to lay out on their stomachs with guns aimed at their heads. Eight people were held outside while they raided Lamar's mom house. They had been watching her house for over two weeks. Lamar had a feeling they were being watched because of all the unusual vehicles he saw in the area and people walking up and down the block. That was why he didn't make any sales in front of his house, but when Phillip and Triangle arrived in the Cadillac on rims and handed him the paper bags, they became suspicious and rushed in hoping they had Lamar's supplier, but they found nothing but some food and a little money.

CHAPTER 20

After being asked a hundred questions, Phillip and Triangle were finally allowed to leave.

"So, that's the type of guys you deal with?" Phillip asked her, when they were in the car and on their way.

Triangle was embarrassed at what happened. "Things happen Uncle and they didn't even find anything," she said, trying to explain everything away as accidental.

Phillip looked over at her with surprise. "Don't try to bull shit me! Why didn't you tell me he sold drugs?"

"U..um, I don't know. I didn't think it was very important."

"You didn't think putting me or yourself in harm's way wasn't important? That's your boyfriend right?"

"Yeah," she answered looking down at her phone again, as David called her. What she didn't know was that David discovered the 3 bodies in the van after they started stinking the garage up. He called the police and had already ratted out Triangle as the driver of the van. He was trying to get in touch with her now and have her arrested.

"Well, selling drugs is very dangerous, especially when a person is being flashy like that. You don't ever want to be in love with a nigga' that's flashy like that when he's doing something illegal. It's a red flag that says come arrest me. That's what idiots do," Phillip told her, trying to smarten her up before it was too late.

"What's wrong with being flashy if you got it?" Triangle asked, being stubborn again, trying to defend Lamar.

"Let's say you and Lamar stayed together, or you just simply riding together in his car. By him being so flashy, he will have most likely made himself a target, whether it's the stick-up kids that want him or the police."

"What's that got to do with me?"

Looking at her and shaking his head at her attitude he said, "A lot! You can be in the middle of a shooting, you can be kidnapped and held hostage until Lamar pays so much money to get you back before they kill you. They can kill someone close to you like me who don't know what's up. It's a lot to think about when you're dealing with a nigga' like that. Trust me, I've been there when I was younger. I use to always be flashing my stuff, showing off my jewelry, nice clothes and fancy cars. The stick-up kids and other jealous people in my city wanted me dead, but they could hardly ever get to me, so you know what they did?"

"What they do uncle?" Triangle asked, absorbed into his story that showed another side of him she didn't know existed.

"They caught my daughter Julie, Jacky, and your aunt leaving school. They kidnapped all of them and asked me to pay $100,000. Something I didn't have. I just made it look like I had it like that with the cars I was driving," Phillip told her, watching her eyes turn as big saucers.

"Oh my god! Are you serious?" Triangle was shocked. Her grandma had never told her anything like that.

"Yup, and on top of that, when I finally came up with the $100,000, I got my family back, but they all had been raped by five different guys, and it was all my fault. So you have to watch the people you deal with and also watch what you do, because if a person can't get to you they will get the closest person to you, and if you think I'm lying about anything, look what recently happened to your cousin Keeymo. He got robbed, they put him in the trunk, drove him around to get more money after they had just took over $200,000 from him. They was gonna kill him until he took them to his mother's house at two in the morning. He gave them $30,000 and they still shot him in the stomach twice. He's alive but do you see what I mean?" Phillip asked after telling her the details.

"Dang, yeah! I didn't know all that comes with messing around with a drug dealer."

"Yeah I know. No one thinks about the consequences until it's too late. That's why I'm telling you and that's not even the half of it. There are many things I've been through with my wife, it's crazy, and we both should have been dead a long time ago."

"Well, what am I supposed to do, be gay?" Triangle asked, being a smart ass.

"What you mean?" Phillip asked, confused.

"Every boy I know sells drugs," she said, explaining what she meant.

"Damn, you serious?" he asked looking at her to see if she was pulling his leg again.

"Yeah, every boy I talk to is always like, I had these clothes on for five days or they just be like I'm about to hit the block."

Phillip laughed, "Okay, well you have to search outside of your city or state, because there's positive guys out there, trust me."

"But they too far away and why I gotta go find them?" she asked, not too happy about leaving her area.

"Where does it say you have to have a boyfriend to define you? That's not important. What's important is that you get yourself together first. Don't try to love someone else when you're not sure if you love yourself." Phillip told her, getting pretty deep to the root of her life.

CHAPTER 21

When they arrived back at Phil's house, David was still calling her, texting her and leaving voicemails. Triangle just knew he was pissed off about his car and her not coming home last night. Soon as she got out of the truck she went upstairs inside her uncle's house and called David.

"Hello!" he answered quickly, "Oh my God, I thought you were dead! Where are you?" he asked. The police was right there recording everything he said plus tracking Triangle's cell phone location. They had collected finger prints off the van and all they had to do was take her in and match her prints then charge her with all three murders.

"Calm down, I'm fine," she told him.

"Well when are you going to bring me my car?"

"Tonight I'll bring it."

"Can you come right now? I really wanna see you and I wanna… never mind," he said, cutting himself off short after the police gave him a signal that he sounded too phony and desperate. They had her location and her phone tapped. The only way they could lose her was if she turned her phone off or she broke it.

"No I can't come right now, I'm at my uncles. I'll be there later on, ok."

"Ok, well I will see you then."

"Oh I have a situation, but I'll pay for it or work it off somehow," she said, in a freaky tone of voice.

David laughed, "Naw you don't have to worry, whatever happened to the car, its covered honey."

"Ok cool!" she said with excitement.

"Ok, I guess I will see you later then."

"Yep, you will."

Later that night Triangle left her uncle's house and headed to David's place. She had no idea the police was waiting for her. When she arrived, everything looked normal and she still had no clue. She was expecting a black eye or two. She felt that she deserved it and it wouldn't be too bad for causing thousands of dollars in damages. Soon as she opened the door and stepped one foot out the car the police came out from everywhere. She was blocked in by 4 patrol cars and still she had no clue what was going on.

"Put your fucking hands up now!" the officer yelled. Triangle did just that and that's when they rushed in on her throwing her to the ground and cuffing her.

"Damn, calm down, what the hell I do so bad you have to throw me around?"

"Shut up, you have the right to remain silent, anything you say will be used against you in the court of law."

"What I do? What am I being charged with?" she asked, now scared and shaking.

"Murder," one cop said, "You are under arrest for first degree murder."

Triangle's eyes grew big. "Murder? I didn't murder anyone!" she shouted, now wiggling around.

"Tell it to the judge."

Triangle was arrested and taken down to the police station where they put her in a holding cell with 9 other people. She slept on concrete all night and was unable to eat the breakfast they served her when she woke up. She was just ready to go to court. After she came back from court, she found out she was being charged with three murders and she was looking at natural life with no chance of parole. That scared the hell out of her. She kept asking the guards if she can talk to a detective. It took hours for her to be pulled out the cell, but when the detectives came and got her she was relieved and happy. "So how are you Ms.Kingmon? You're looking at a lot of time. Is there anything you want to tell us?" one of the detectives asked.

She swallowed hard and was so scared. She began thinking to herself and knowing there was no way on earth she could do three natural life sentences, but she did not want to tell on Ant. "Is there any way I can get out of this? I can't do the rest of my life in here," she finally said.

"Well did you kill these people?"

"Hell no!" she shouted.

"I believe her Jack," the Mexican detective said to the white one.

"She's full of shit, look at her, she looks like a murderer," he said, sounding serious but he didn't really mean it.

"No, not me. You guys have the wrong person," she said.

CHAPTER 22

"Well who's the right person or people?" Jack asked.

Triangle did not give up Ant's name, although the detectives had already picked him up and questioned him because the van was previously in his name. Ant told them that he did not know what was going on and that he had sold the van years ago. They had nothing really on him, so they let him go and was going to do further investigation, Ant already switched everything out of his name. Triangle did make a huge deal with the feds with a black detective that stayed in Saginaw, Michigan. She was escorted to his house and that's where she had to stay for a week straight to be trained for how to set the bad guys up. She was scared, but she cared about nothing at this point. She didn't want to tell on Ant and she was sure that she didn't want to do life.

"Hi, how are you? My name is Detective Shed, I will be working with you and giving you your assignments. You have a lot of work to do. I'm going to have to hook you up with a tether to keep track of you. You have no curfew, this is only for tracking purposes. You will stay here for a week learning tricks to get information out of people. You will live basically a normal life, but you will always be turning in people and setting them up. I want drug dealers, murderers, rapist, etc. Any questions?"

"How many people do I have to turn in before I'm done?"

"A lot, so don't worry about that right now. I'll let you know when you are done. You will be provided with housing and transportation by us. The more drug bust you get us, the better your lifestyle will get. Anymore questions?"

Triangle was speechless. She was down for whatever, she planned to meet all kind of people and bust them. She liked talking to Detective Shed.

Triangle had been there over 4 days now and today was her last full day as she was sitting on the couch alone with Shed telling her about the dangers of the jobs she would have to do.

"Can you show me some defense moves?" she asked really just wanting to be close to him, she thought he was so sexy.

"Ah, sure why not? Stand up," he told her, as he began showing her different ways to get out of different things. He felt Triangle trying to flirt with him, rubbing against him with her booty. He had dealt with this plenty of times. Triangle knew exactly what she was doing while wearing some white booty shorts and a tank top.

"You think you can handle all this ass? Your wife don't have all this," she said.

"Now that will get you back in jail. Don't say anything about my wife."

"Sorry! Well, can you handle this?" she asked, pressing up against him.

"I'm not interested."

"I won't tell a soul, I promise," she said pulling down her shorts and panties.

"Put your clothes back on please."

"Why? You know you want me, it's written all over your face. Like I said, I won't tell on you."

Detective Shed thought hard and long. He believed she wouldn't tell, especially if she didn't tell on the murderer to get herself out of trouble. He had done this with plenty of his clients and she was by far the prettiest and sexiest of them all and she was now standing butt ass naked right in front of him.

"Come on Shed, handcuff me. I'm under arrest, right?" she said, as she turned around and bent over spreading her ass cheeks showing her pussy. "This pussy is safe, you don't even need a condom for this pussy, and I just got checked recently, it's clean and wet just for you."

"Look, I don't know what the hell you up to, but you have a lot of work to do, so I suggest you put back on your clothes," he said.

"So you telling me you don't want to fuck me?"

Silence…

CHAPTER 23

"Hello, Mr. Shed," she said, as she began playing with his belt buckle and he didn't stop her. *Damn he looks like Morris Chestnut*, she thought to herself.

"I won't unbuckle you if you don't want it. So tell me, do you want this pussy or not?" she asked, yanking softly on his belt. She could see the print of his penis through his jeans, his dick was rock hard. "Wow you have a huge dick," she said, gripping it through his pants.

"I don't think I had nothing this big before, is that real?" She was really shocked at how big his dick was. She was now thinking twice about fucking him, he was abnormal.

"Ok, I give up, you can't handle this pussy," she said, turning around getting ready to put her clothes back on until she felt him grab her with force looking her in her eyes.

"I'm not scared of you," she said, looking him back in his eyes with careless written all over her face.

Triangle was beautiful to him, he just wanted to tongue her down. His eyes told her more than he could ever say even though he stayed silent, she knew he wanted to fuck her. She was still naked and he had her by her arm. She took her fingers and ran it between her pussy lips then put them in his mouth. He sucked and licked every bit of juice off her fingers and they started kissing. There was no way Triangle was about to try to suck his dick. She didn't even think that it would fit in her mouth. He kissed her, slobbering all over her soft lips and laid her naked body down on the couch. He tongue kissed her neck and sucked gently on both sides, moving down to her nipples and sucking each one of them. Although he was eager to fuck her, he took his time because he wasn't sure if he wanted to or not. She was young but she had a body like a woman. He sucked all over her then made his way between her thighs, licking her wet and soft pussy lips, then her clit. The taste of her pussy was so good to him, he immediately lost himself. She had no type of odor, she just smelled fresh and clean. He hadn't had pussy like this since he was in high school. He ate her pussy like it was no tomorrow while she laid back screaming his name repeatedly. She was cumming like never before. No one had ever ate her pussy like he was eating it nor as long.

After cumming 5 times in a row, her body felt limp but her pussy juices was flowing like a faucet. There was nut all over the leather couch and Detective Shed didn't seem to care. He just kept licking Triangle's good tasting pussy. He was sucking the life out of her and soon she felt another orgasm building up. "Oh shit, here I cum!" she shouted biting her bottom lip and grabbing his head while squeezing her shaking thighs together. "Oh my god! I feel it!" she shouted louder. "Shed, baby! Damn!" she kept screaming and shouting until she pushed out another nut. She was breathing hard and sweating but she wasn't going to tell him to stop. His head game was rare and she'd probably never get it again like this so she laid there and enjoyed herself. She didn't care if this went for days, he was the best with his tongue. He had her so wet, she wasn't worrying about how big his dick was anymore, she was more than ready. She seen him still licking and sucking her pussy while taking his clothes off, his dick was like the size of her forearm. She was unable to put inches on that. He was more like a foot. She asked herself over and over, why and how was a person's dick able to be that big. Whatever the answer was to that question was irrelevant because she felt her body shaking again ready to burst. This time she felt light headed. "S..H..E.E.D!" she moaned while squirting nut like she had a water gun between her legs. She then felt him lifting her legs back all the way to her head now licking all around her asshole. "What… the….fuck!" she said biting her lip and squeezing her titties. She could not believe what was happening and she could barely catch her breath. This was over board, but it felt like a dream. Everything between her legs was soaking wet, yet there was still no smell at all. He licked and sucked her ass until she was screaming his name loudly and pulling her own hair nearly out. "Wa…it! Wait! Please!" She screamed until he stopped and looked at her. He had wetness all over his face. "What are you trying to do to me?" she asked, getting off the couch but soon realized she couldn't walk. Her knees buckled right away and she could do nothing but fall. "Oh my god, I can't walk, what are you trying to do to me?" she asked confused, but feeling like she was floating.

"Nothing, I thought this was what you wanted. You didn't even let me finish yet, come here," he said, walking towards her.

"No, get away from me, I'm good! You have put it all the way down. I can't go no more."

He smiled while he stared at her looking so helpless while curled up on the floor. "Okay let me put you to bed, that's enough for you for today," he said, going over to her, picking her up and carrying her upstairs to his bedroom instead of the guest room where she slept. She didn't realize it because he was kissing her so good and deeply the whole way, by the time they got to his bed she was ready for some more. Shed whole arm was wet from her pussy when he laid her down. "Damn this pussy is leaking."

"Eat me some more," she said in a sexy voice.

He dove his face right in. She was really leaking juices. Now it was time for her to get the real thing. Shed licked and fingered her for a few more seconds while rubbing her juices all over his long hard dick. He then kissed all the way up her body to her neck then her ears. He whispered in her ear while her eyes were closed. "Here I come," he said as he slid his dick slowly inside her.

She took a deep breath as she felt him easing in slowly. She wondered how deep he was going until she felt him deep inside her pussy, then her stomach, chest and back. "f.....u....c..k! Sh...iiiii..tt!" she moaned turning her head left and right and closing her eyes tightly. His dick filled her whole body and it still felt like he was shoving more inside her.

He stroked softly making sure she felt all good pain. "You ok?" he whispered, pumping slowly as his whole dick was inside of her rubbing against her wet soft walls. He knew he could punish her for talking shit but he wasn't going to. He was enjoying her pussy and he planned on fucking her the whole time she was working for him.

"Yes... yes! You so fucking BIG! Damn!" she moaned. "Go faster," she said in a soft voice now getting used to feeling him inside of her.

He pumped a little faster but not too fast, he didn't want to hurt her, but he finally had her digging her nails in his back and screaming.

"Ah! Ah! Ah! Fuck! Me! Ah! Yes!" She shouted, as he pumped inside her getting faster and faster. Her legs was over his shoulders and he was deep in her pussy, plugging her in and out while she yelled his name and squeezed his booty cheeks with her nails. "Stay deep baby! Stay deep! I feel it! Stay deep! Its cumming baby! Stay deep!" she shouted. He continued to pump and pump, barely coming out of her. He kept his dick deep inside her until he felt her shake. He sped up when her eyes started rolling then got on his feet and really started hitting the bottom of her pussy. Her moans turned into screams and it sounded like she was being raped. He beat that pussy up for about 15 seconds straight long deep, fast and hard strokes until he came inside her.

They both collapsed and Shed was still deep inside her while sucking on the side of her neck. He couldn't help but put a hickie on her. The sex was phenomenal. "You ok?" he asked still deep inside her, hard as a rock and still leaking cum.

She took a deep breath before saying, "Yes, wow you are the shit. Don't take your dick out of me, we doing it again," she said with sweat all above her lips and her face.

He smiled showing his pretty white teeth. "So you like this dick huh?"

"That is not a dick, that's a bat," she joked and they both laughed.

"Can you still feel me?" he asked.

"Hell yeah, I can feel you all in me. You like touching my back right now, but it feel good now. At first that shit was feeling weird, but now I like it especially when you go deep."

"Good, because you gonna be getting this dick often. You got some bomb ass pussy and it taste brand new."

"Thank you," she said, blushing.

They fucked for more hours then got up, changing sheets and wiping down the couch that had nut all over it. Triangle was so tired and wore out, she couldn't wait to take a nap. She made it to sleep 20 minutes before Shed wife got home from a long day at work.

CHAPTER 24

The next morning after Detective Shed's wife went to work, it was time to get Triangle up and ready, her first mission started today which was to get in good with a dealer name Bonus. Shed knew her job would be much easier to do since she had lots of sex appeal. That itself would draw her victims towards her.

Triangle just sat on the bed thinking to herself how great Shed was, but she knew right now there was more important stuff she had to do and that was getting herself out of all the trouble she was in. She thought about escaping and trying to leave the country but she was scared.

As soon as Shed got out the shower, Triangle made her way to the shower and they both went shopping for some linens afterwards. He took her to the mall and brought her a few outfits to hold her over. He then gave her some money, gave her keys to an Envoy SUV, then he dropped her off at a hotel that was located in Frankenmuth City, right by an outlet called Birch Run.

"This is where you gonna be staying. This is the truck I just gave you the keys to. It's a good vehicle so you don't have to worry about being stranded. Oh and there's no dead bodies in the back neither," he said.

Triangle didn't find it funny though. "How long do I have to stay here?"

"I don't know yet."

"I gotta stay here all by myself?"

"Yep, but you would be under surveillance 24/7. There's camera's inside the room so that you have no company and there's an officer sitting outside watching not only the area, but you as well. Don't do anything stupid."

Triangle shook her head and seen her life being a living hell. "So what am I supposed to do?"

"Be patient, everything is up in your room. You have your wires that you will be wearing. There's a DVD you must watch on how to use different gadgets. Then you have a folder on your bed that tells you everything you must do, but to sum all of that up, just call me. The first person is Bonus. All you have to do is get as close as possible to him. He's already being watched, but we need someone inside. Today he supposed to be at the mall with his son.

Hopefully you can push up on them." Shed said, as he finally parked in a parking spot close to the door of the hotel.

"So just get to know him?"

"Basically, but you have to do some snooping around. No sex, just investigation. Meet who you can and find out what you can, and we will do the rest. The car has a tracking on it and the cell phone you have does too, so buy a personal phone for yourself. Live your life the same don't over think anything. Everything is still the same, you are just working for us. There's no rush on nothing, just patience. Any extra dealers you meet will just be a plus and of course it will help you out, but our main focus are the guys that are in the folder. Go at your own speed and don't drop the ball."

"Ok, I think I got it. What if I see a bunch of drugs?"

"Call me and let me know."

"Ok," she said, not really understanding her position. She knew Shed wasn't telling her everything but she was going to do whatever she needed to. She got out of the car and went to her room. It was on the third floor. Soon as she got inside she noticed that it was a nice room. She went straight to the folder and started reading. She found out more than Shed told her. She didn't know she had to pose as a female drug dealer. She knew nothing about selling drugs, but there was plenty dvd's inside the room for her to practice with. She planned to watch them later, but right now she had to be at a mall that was located in Detroit in less than two hours. She had a long drive. She was also directed to a duffle bag that had money inside of it that was marked. This was money only to buy drugs with and nothing else. Shed had promised her $500 a week for spending money as well. She counted the money up and she had thirty thousand dollars cash.

CHAPTER 25

Soon she was out the door and her mission was to meet Bonus, get close to him and buy a Kilo of cocaine from him. She looked at this as simple. She drove all the way Detroit by herself. She wanted to pick up Sincere but she wanted to catch her when she wasn't at her home. Triangle knew her dad was a big drug dealer and she didn't want to put him in her mess.

Later as she was walking through the mall she found no one that looked like the picture Shed had. This was much harder than she thought so she called Shed to find out Bonus location. He told her and she went straight to the store he was at with his son just like Shed told her. They were both trying on shoes when Triangle walked in wearing a white dress with some white heels and a purse to match.

When she seen her target she wasted no time, she walked right over to them. "I love them shoe's!" she said, smiling showing her pretty teeth. "Those are cute, I want to buy my little brother some of those," she said.

Bonus looked up and was shocked. Triangle was sexy and he was already undressing her and imagining himself sleeping with her. "You like these huh?"

"Yes, these are cute," she said, grabbing one off the floor and looking at it. She had no interest in the shoe but she was hoping that her strategy would work. "Are you about to get these?" she said looking inside at the size.

"Yeah, now I am since you like them," Bonus said, smiling. His son was just looking at him still trying on his shoes.

"What that mean?" she asked, looking him in his eyes.

"Exactly how it sounds lil mama."

"I'm Triangle."

"Oh, I'm sorry Triangle," he said, silent for a moment just staring at her.

"Are you from around here?"

"Nope, are you?"

"Yeah, I'm from the city. You need to fuck with a nigga," he said.

"Really?"

"Yeah, really."

"Why is that?" she asked, moving a little closer to him. She didn't know how well the speaker was, she had to make sure it could hear him.

"Because I'm that guy," he said, reaching in his back pocket and handing her one of his cards. She read it and it said something about a modeling agency.

"I could get you out there. You look like the model type and these niggas around here will love you."

"Thanks but, I'm not into modeling. I'm into getting real money in these streets," she said.

"Oh for real? Well you already know what it is on that tip, that's nothing lil mama."

"Triangle."

"Damn my bad, I'm used to saying that shit."

"Well get use to saying Triangle, because I'll be calling you about that business," she said, sounding like a rookie in the game, which she was. She tried to walk away but he grabbed her arm.

"Bitch is you the police or a set up bitch?"

Oh my god, how did he know, she thought to herself. "No, nigga! What the fuck, let go of me!" she said, snatching away from him.

"Give me that card back," he said.

Triangle was confused and she thought he was on to her. "Why?"

"Because I'ma give you my personal number to call me about that."

Triangle was now able to breathe. "Oh ok."

He gave her his number and told her to call him. She walked out the store nervous and knowing she was too much of an amateur to be a drug dealer. She was starting to wonder why they even gave her that mission. She knew she either had to learn fast or she would probably get killed. Bonus grabbing her arm as hard as he did woke her up and let her know that everything was realer than she thought. She drove all the way back to her hotel room and began watching some of the DVD's. The first one she watched was a movie called "Paid in full." She watched it four times in a row and she kept trying to imitate the way Cameron (Rico) was acting. Although he was flashy she loved his swag and the way he didn't play no games. All she had to do was switch it around and do the things he was doing from a woman's perspective. She just had to become a lot braver. She was in the mirror practicing acting like she was holding a gun. She was mad that they didn't give her a gun. *How do they expect me to be a drug dealer without a gun,* she thought, but then she thought again and realized since they will be watching her 24/7 they had her covered.

CHAPTER 26

Triangle phone was ringing and she did not recognize the number. "Hello?"

"Triangle, whatsup baby?"

"Who is this?"

"Bonus, the nigga that was about to beat ya ass at the mall," he joked.

She laughed, "Oh, hey. I'm sorry about that. I just don't like beating around the bush about what I do," she said.

"Well that's how you get caught, you not supposed to expose shit like that. I only grabbed you like that to put fear in your heart. I know you not the police, I was just messing with you, but I coulda been the police and you woulda been done for," he said.

"You right."

"But when can I see you? I'll put you up on game and tell you how this shit work if you want me to. I can see you young and you just now getting into the game, but you have to learn some of the rules of this shit especially if you trying to get real money. I don't do much talking on the phone so we gonna have to meet up somewhere. You want to go out tonight?"

"Yeah, sure."

"Um, yeah. I got a friend I may bring," she said.

Triangle had no clue where he was talking about but she was about to find out. He gave her directions to a strip club on 8mile road and she was going to use the navigation on her phone. She called Sincere as soon as she hung up.

2 months later.

Triangle had stepped her game up and she was doing her thing posing as a drug dealer. Her and Shed would meet at the hotel room and usually have sex in a separate room or in one of the lobby bathrooms. She had been buying from Bonus and everything was going good. She was on to the next mission and everything was becoming easy. She had now watched over ten drug dealing movies multiple times and she was getting the hang of it, well at least, going to buy it. She didn't have to sell anything so she put all her energy towards getting close to the dealers.

Her next mission was to buy five kilos from a guy that was back and forth from Texas. She was to meet him at a restaurant he loved eating at. That would be the easiest way because of the way he moved.

The day came when she seen his BMW parked at the restaurant. She parked near him and went in, dressed to impress. She was making more money now and she was treating Sincere to a meal. Sincere was also dressed to impress and she was looking good as well. She had no idea what Triangle was up to.

They both walked in and was seated nowhere near her target. The only way Triangle could see him was when she went to the bathroom. She noticed he was fat and Mexican. She had no idea how she would get over to him, but she knew she had to come up with something. So when she got back to the table she wrote a note in Spanish and gave it to her waitress to take over to him while she was eating.

"Girl, so I met this guy name Kiwi," Sincere said, with a big smile on her face.

"Kiwi? Is he cute?"

"Of course! And he has green eyes."

"He's black?"

"White."

"Hell naw, they crazy girl. Trust me, leave him alone."

Sincere laughed taking a drink from her straw. "That's not all white guys. That's just the ones you was dealing with. Do you still mess around with him?"

"Nooo, hell no."

Sincere laughed. "Well this one is different. He's a boss girl. He knows my dad and…" Sincere stopped talking when she seen Triangle moving back from the table holding her chest. "You ok?"

"Yeah, just a heart burn," she said, going to the bathroom. She didn't want Sincere's dad being on the radar so she went in the bathroom and took her wire off. It wasn't needed right now anyway. She came back and noticed he was writing. She was hoping it was for her.

CHAPTER 27

"You sure you ok?"

"Yeah Sincere, I'm good. Finish telling me about your friend."

"Ok," Sincere smiled and got comfortable. "So he deals with my dad and he's been coming over lately and I seen him looking at me, so when my dad wasn't around, I said hi and it went from there, but that was the first interaction with him and we wasn't able to exchange numbers because my dad came back."

"Do you think he knows what's going on?"

"No."

"So?"

"So, he took me out yesterday and we kissed for the first time and it felt so right."

Triangle just looked at her then a thought popped in her head. She didn't care about what Sincere was saying, she had a lot of work to do or else her life was over. "Does he have friends?"

"I'm not sure. Do you want me to ask? I'm sure he could hook you up with someone. He has money girl."

"I'm sure he does."

Soon the waitress came back to the table and passed Triangle a note from El Migo. He told her to come over to the table.

"I'll be right back."

"Where you going?" Sincere asked. Triangle had been to the bathroom more than twice so she knew something wasn't right.

"Just chill," Triangle said, walking right over and sitting down at El Migo's table. She noticed his face right away and was disgusted. She now knew why he sat alone. He had pimples all over his face and you could tell he picked with them. She didn't understand why he just wouldn't go to the doctor and spend some money to get it taken care of.

"Hi," she said, with a small smile.

"How are you? Do I know you?"

"No, but you can."

He smiled, "So?"

"Oh. You looked so… cute so I just thought I would say hi."

"Thanks mami," he said with his raspy voice. "Are you from around here?"

"I live in Pontiac, you?"

"Dearborn. I stay in Dearborn."

"You married?" she asked, already knowing he was.

"Yes, but it's one thing to be married and to be happily married."

"That sucks," she said.

"Yeah, big time."

"So are you able to have friends on the side?"

"Yeah, I'll take your number down and I'll contact you, say tonight?" he said.

She smiled, "Don't get it twisted, I don't do night parties unless it's about money."

"Money's no problem."

"I'm a business woman."

Triangle had just remembered that she didn't have her wire on, but she continued anyway. "I don't know if you the police or not, so I rather not say."

"Ohh, that kind of business woman huh?" he said, looking around.

She smiled to assure him that she was in the same business as he was. "You can give me a call in the day time and maybe we can go out for some brunch," she said, as she slid her number over to him.

El Migo liked her style. She seemed as if she had class and she was drop dead gorgeous, he didn't want her to leave. He was use to buying girls that looked like her and he was confident that he could buy her panties right off her. "How much? Stop the games."

"How much for what?" she asked.

"For you."

"I'm not for sale. Besides you couldn't afford me."

He laughed and sat back sucking on his toothpick. "So you just come to my table to tease me?" he asked.

"I'm not teasing, I'm just looking for something specific and so are you."

"What are you trying to find?"

"A good man."

"Well I'm married. Anything else?"

"You sure you not the police?"

"Mami, come one, be serious, I have an ounce of coke in my pocket right now that I have been snorting all day. I'm not the police."

"I need five kilos," she said.

El Migo leaned forward and said, "I can't help you."

"Alright," she said standing up and walking away switching her hips from side to side.

El Migo looked and could not let her go, "Wait, come here," he said, waving his hands towards her. She turned around and came back to the table. "I might can get them for you, you just have to make sure you have the cash."

CHAPTER 28

A month later she was buying from Bonus and El Migo.
A case was built on Bonus and he was indicted quickly, ,
facing life if he went to trial. However he had a deal on the
table for 20 years. He was told that he sold to the police but
he still had no clue it was Triangle. Since he didn't go to
trial she didn't have to show her face by getting on the
stand and pointing him out. El Migo loved doing business
with her because she was consistent. She always called him
for what she needed and he kept trying to have sex with
her. About three months later, she called him for ten kilos
and that's when he was arrested. Triangle was on the roll
and she was on her way to bigger and more dangerous drug
dealers. She had been on vacation for two weeks now and
went home to visit her grandmother and gave her $2000
dollars. Her grandmother noticed that she had matured a
lot and she was growing up. She told her grandmother that
she had her own place and car and she was working as a
secretary. She also went to see her uncle to get some tips
about men.

She had been calling Detective Shed from both her phones but he wasn't answering. Since she was on vacation, he was spending time with his wife. Triangle drove over to his house and parked down the street. It was dark out and she got out, wearing some sweat pants, a belly shirt, and some sneakers. She crept up to the side window to look inside but the blinds were closed. Soon, a light flashed on and she ran to the back of the house. She tried dialing Shed number again and he answered. "What is your problem? You think I don't know where you at? Get the hell out of here," he whispered loudly.

Triangle couldn't say anything besides, "I need to see you."

"Get the fuck out of here for I have your ass thrown in jail Triangle." That scared her so she hung up and walked back to the SUV crying. She realized she had no power or privacy. He knew her whereabouts at all times. She was hurt and didn't know what to do. She drove all the way to Pontiac and she finally made up her mind to call Ant. The number was disconnected, so she called Brisco and he answered.

"Hello."

"Heey, this Triangle."

"Who?"

"Triangle."

"Oh, whatsup girl, how you been? I been trying to get in touch with you."

"I been good, I just had a lot going on that's all."

"Damn, I thought something bad happened to you or something."

"No, I'm good. Are you busy right now?"

"Naw, I'm just chilling, are you trying to come through or something?"

She laughed, "Yeah, I am."

"Whats funny?"

"You, guessing what I'm up to like you know me or something."

"Oh I know you very well," he told her. "Do you even remember where I live?" he joked.

She laughed, "Shut up, I'll be there in a minute nigga."

"Alright."

She arrived at his house fifteen minutes later and they sat and talked for a while. Brisco could tell that there was something different about her. She wasn't the same. It almost was like she was going through something. He sensed that her vibe was way more serious than before. He asked her was everything alright, but she told him she was fine and he let it be.

Later that night, they were still lying on the couch cuddled up and Triangle was falling asleep. Brisco wanted to fuck so he started playing with her pussy working his fingers on her clit until her pussy was dripping wet. He heard her moan and he watched as her eyes opened wide and a small smile appeared on her face. "You nasty," she said, "Who said you can touch that?"

"You did," he said, kissing her in the mouth. They begin tongue kissing and stripping their clothes off slowly. Brisco started kissing her stomach and he made his way all the way down to her pussy lips. He ate her out for thirty minutes straight, making her cum twice before he was sticking his dick inside her. It slipped right in and for a minute he was thinking she was just super wet but soon he realized her pussy was not the same. He remembered when it was tight and wet, now it was loose and wet. He stroked about ten times and he couldn't feel much so he slid out and tried to put it in her ass, but she stopped him.

"No we not going there," she said, with her hand on his stomach.

"Why not?"

"Because I'm not in the mood for all that Brisco."

He didn't say nothing, he just turned her over and started pounding her pussy from the doggy style position until he came. He pulled out and nutted all over her back then he went to the bathroom. He was known to go half the night inside her but he was done after the first nut. She got herself back dressed and when he came back she was curled up lying on the couch.

"What's wrong?" he asked.

"Nothing. What's wrong with you?"

"Nothing, why you say that?" he asked, sitting beside her.

"You never fucked me that quick before."

"It be like that sometimes."

"Whatever."

"That shit ain't the same Triangle, you been fucking too many niggas or something."

She raised up, "What you mean?"

"That shit ain't tight like it used to be."

"What?" she said, with a confused look on her face. She was embarrassed.

"You been fucking too much or something or you just been fucking a nigga with a big ass dick. I couldn't feel shit. Your shit use to be cushion inside. That shit was whack ass hell."

CHAPTER 29

"You muthafucka! You don't have to be so disrespectful!" She got up and headed for the door. Brisco didn't stop her, he wasn't happy at all and he wanted her to leave. "See if you ever fuck me again!" she said, slamming his door. She raced to the SUV and as soon as she got in she bust out in tears.

She and drove away seconds later, trying to stop herself from crying. She wanted to go back to her hotel room to be alone, but she didn't want to drive that far. Her plan was to just stay at her grandma house for the night after she got herself something to eat. She went to the Coney Island and by surprise she seen a familiar face in front of her. He seen her first through his side mirror and started blowing his horn to get her attention. At first she was trying not to be seen, but she gave in because she knew he wasn't about to let her just go. She started waving and smiling but he wanted her to pull over to the side after she got her food. She did just that and she put her window down for him.

"Where the fuck you been?" he asked.

She smiled, "Around, where have you been?"

"Looking for you, you looking good too you know they never brought up charges on me for the shit that happened."

"Yeah, I know."

"I thought you was going to tell on me. That was real shit."

She just smiled and opened up her food getting ready to eat, she was starving.

"What you got up for the night? You trying to play or what? I miss that pussy."

"Ant please, you don't miss shit. You had me fucking everybody."

"That was when my money was fucked up, I'm good now, and I'm just trying to fuck with you tonight."

"You still stay at the same place?"

"Naw, I got a new spot on the east side. You gonna come through?"

"I guess," she said, knowing he was gonna want to fuck so she checked her glove department for her baby wipes.

"Just follow me out of here then," he said, backing out.

She shook her head ok as she was raising her window. She followed him home and when they arrived he went in and she told him to hold up. She had to clean herself up. When she was done she went in with her food although she wasn't really hungry anymore. She was glad to see Ant. She had missed him. He was the person she loved the most.

"What's your new number?" she asked, handing him her phone. "It's funny because I was actually trying to call you earlier tonight and I wind up running right into you."

"You tried to call me?"

"Yeah, are you surprised?"

"A little, it's been a minute since I seen you. You looking good too. I see you done got thicker. I see somebody been on their job. You got a new nigga?"

"Something like that."

He laughed as he started breaking down a blunt and rolling some weed into it. They drinked and smoked about four blunts before he had her in his room fucking her. He noticed that her pussy was different also but he continued to fuck her and nut in her. They fucked until the sun rise and then they went to sleep. Triangle slept until two o' clock in the afternoon and when she woke up she heard guys talking in the other room. She could hear Ant talking about her and how much he was going to charge them to fuck her. She got up and went to the bathroom.

"Triangle!"

"What? I'm about to brush my teeth!"

Ant went into the bathroom and closed it. "Look, I got these niggas out here ready to spend some money, what's up?"

She shook her head, "No Ant, I'm not with that no more. I gotta go anyways."

CHAPTER 30

He wanted to slap her, but he just left out and slammed the door. She knew he was mad but she didn't care. When she came back out Ant was in the room lying on the bed watching Tv. "You know you coulda did that for me."

"I'm not like that no more."

"Whatever! You got some money?" he asked seeing if she was going to lie to him. He had already looked in her purse.

"Yeah, why?"

"I need a couple hundred."

"I thought you said you had your money right now."

"I do, I'm just trying to do something. You gonna let me get it or not?" he asked, ready to take it from her if she denied him.

"I don't care." She looked in her purse and pulled out some money and counted out two hundred dollars in twenty dollar bills.

"Where you get all that from?"

"I work now Ant. I have a job that pays well."

He didn't bother asking where she worked because he didn't care. He just took the money she was giving him. "Thanks, I gotta go though. How long it's gonna take you to get dressed?"

"I'm dressed right now, I didn't bring clothes. You ready for me to leave?"

"Yeah I got to go."

"My pussy still good to you?"

Ant looked at her wondering if she had read his mind. Which was no. "Umm, it's straight, I could tell you been fucking a lot though. It used to be real tight."

"It's loose now?" she asked.

She became mad again, not at Ant but at Shed. His dick was bigger than anyone she ever had sex with and now all the people that use to love her pussy had a different outlook on it. She didn't know what to do. She was quiet as she got herself together and left. She called her uncle and told him she needed to talk to him.

She arrived at her uncle's house and her hair was all over her head. She did her best trying to fix it before she went inside, but her uncle could tell she had just got through from doing the nasty.

"Whatsup beautiful? Where you coming from?"

"A friend house."

"You hungry? I got some chicken in there I just fried about an hour ago."

"Naw, I'm good. I just stopped by to talk to you for a second," she said, as she sat on the couch.

"Is everything alright? I hope you not doing anything illegal to get the money you have now."

"I'm not, I have a job."

"Ok, what is it on your mind?"

"Don't judge me uncle, but what is a girl supposed to do if a guy tell her that she is loose?"

"Loose how?"

"You know, like her vagina."

He took a deep swallow and his eyebrows went down. He had been asked some weird and off the wall questions from his daughter but nothing this awkward. He could tell she was hurt and wounded by the comment and he was going to be gentle with her on this topic although he wanted to curse her out and tell her to keep her legs closed. "Well, I'll tell you this, you can close that hole back up by soaking in some hot bath water with vinegar inside it or you can just stop having sex for a while until it closes back up. I'm also going to tell you this. As long as you having sex with one person, you won't have to worry about that. He would be use to how you normally feel. Now when you jumping around from nigga to nigga, that's when stuff like that is said."

He hit it right on the nose, exactly what she was doing. "Right, thanks," she said.

They talked for about an hour before Triangle was on her way to her hotel room to try what her uncle told her. She made sure she stopped at the store and picked up a couple bottles of vinegar.

CHAPTER 31

The next morning when Triangle woke up inside her hotel Shed was sitting in the chair watching her.

"What the hell are you doing in here?" she said, as she jumped up with the cover over her body.

"Why were you at my house unannounced? Don't you understand I'm married? What are you trying to do, ruin my marriage?" he asked calmly, still sitting in his seat.

Triangle seen the anger in his eyes but she wasn't worried because there was a camera rolling 24 hours inside her room. She shook her head no. "No I'm not trying to ruin nothing. You are ruining me."

"How? I'm saving you, not many people get off murder like this Triangle."

She was silent.

"You can't be doing that shit. There is a tracker on your vehicle and more than just me is watching you. I got calls from three different people this morning asking me questions about why you were in my area last night. What we do has to stay on the hush or it's going to be over for us both."

"I'm sorry, it won't happen again."

"Good. Now let's get down to business."

"No wait, fucking you got my pussy loose to other guys."

"Tell them to grow a bigger dick, that's not my problem."

"It is asshole, if I can't have you when I want, you not going to have the privilege to hit this."

"Privilege? Triangle shut up. Those guys will be ok, they are just trying to put you down because they not packing and when they are inside of you they probably thinking you don't feel nothing because they don't, of course they going to call you loose to prevent you from telling them they have a little dick."

Silence.

"Now to business, I have this one cat. He's in Ohio, so I might have to set you up in a hotel out there which will be good for you because it won't be all these cameras around you. I'll get you a new car to drive and we will go from there."

"I thought I was on a three week vacation?"

"You are, I'm just telling you this now. We're not starting now though. By the way, you are doing a good job."

"Thank you, I'm just trying to keep myself from going to jail."

"Keep this up, you will be taking down big organizations. I know I told you no sex before, but between me and you, you do whatever you have to do to catch these muthafuckas."

Triangle just laughed.

"So what do you have planned for the day?"

"I don't know yet."

"Well I'll holla at you later, I have to go."

Triangle got in the shower and got herself together when Shed left. She got dressed and was ready to get something to eat until she got a call from Sincere. "Hello."

"What you doing?"

"Nothing, about to go get something to eat. Whatsup?" Triangle asked, walking out the door.

"Kiwi has a friend for you girl, he is a big time—"

"Wait Sincere! Um I don't know why I haven't got a new phone yet, this phone is horrible. I'm going to call you back in about an hour, I gotta get a new phone, I can barely hear you girl," Triangle said, before she quickly hung the phone up.

She went to the cell phone store and bought herself a new cell phone, that way she could have her personal conversations without the police hearing.

CHAPTER 32

It took about two hours to call Sincere back but she got around to it.

"Hello."

"Hey, I'm sorry about earlier."

Sincere caught her voice right away. "Damn! Why you hang up on me like that? Then you didn't even answer for me when I called back," Sincere said.

"I'm sorry, my phone was messed up. Save this number in your phone, this is new."

"I was so mad at you. I had to tell you something important."

"Awwww, I'm sorry sweetie," she joked, "Tell me now please."

"Ok, I met Kiwi friend, he's a baller of course and since me and Kiwi was having a fun day, I counted you in and told him we can make it a double date."

"Wait, how did you know I didn't have anything important to do?"

"Triangle are you serious? You are never busy."

Triangle laughed, "Bitch I have a job!"

"Whatever, you not fooling me."

"What's his name and you bet not say, strawberry."

They both laughed.

"No girl, his name is Crews. He's tall, dark and handsome too. Be at my house at five."

"Wait! What should I wear?"

"Well since he's a boss, I'm betting he will have on Gucci or LV, so you might want to step your game up. I'm wearing Chanel."

"Oh my god, I can't afford that right now. If he want me to wear that he can buy it for me," Triangle said, quoting something from her uncle.

"Well, be at my house at five."

"Where we going?"

Triangle was at her house thirty minutes earlier and she was wearing some tight black jeans, a white shirt with some heels and she had on a short girly black leather jacket. Her hair was flat ironed and she was looking good.

"You look cute," Triangle said, smiling.

"You look cute too, what kind of jacket is that? Is that Prada?" she asked, walking over to Triangle trying to look at the tag.

"Girl I paid fifty dollars for this jacket, this is just a regular jacket, nothing major."

"That's cute," Sincere said, with a smile.

"See I don't need all that Prada and Gucci stuff to look cute. If he don't like me like this to hell with him," Triangle said.

"They should be here in a minute. I told him that you are a secretary at a law firm, so just go along with it," Sincere said, looking out the window. "Where is your truck?"

"I parked it up the street."

"Why? My dad don't care."

"I been talking back to some of my ex's and I didn't want to bring no drama to your home, just in case they get on some crazy shit. You know how these niggas is," Triangle said.

"Whatever!" Sincere said, looking out the window. "There they go!" she shouted, stepping back from the window. "I hope they did not see me in that window. How do I look? My hair?"

"Good."

"Lip Gloss? Breath?"

"Horrible, here take some gum."

"Trick!"

"I'm playing!" Triangle said, with a big smile. "You look perfect. What about me?"

"Cute."

"Ok thanks, let's go."

CHAPTER 33

Triangle seen them both outside waiting in a big green Luxury truck. When they got close to the vehicle, Crews stared out from the passenger side looking flawless. He was wearing a Gucci sweater, matching fitted jeans, a Gucci belt, and Gucci Loafers. They hugged him saying her name and he said his then opened the door for her to get in. Sincere and Kiwi sat in the front and they drove off heading to their destination.

"Where we going?" Triangle asked, making herself comfortable. Being around Crews was already intimidating for her. He smelled good and looked good.

"She didn't tell you?" Crews asked, putting one arm on the seat nearly around her.

"No," she lied.

"I know you don't know me well yet, but just trust that you gonna have fun with me today."

"I guess," she said, admiring his nice clean face. His mustache, beard and side burns was all lined up to perfection.

"What that mean?" he asked, with a slight smile.

"Oh nothing. We'll see."

Crews instantly knew there was some ice to break before the rest of the day begin to go good. "So where you from?"

"Pontiac, born and raised. You?"

"I'm from Detroit. Born and raised. I moved to Texas about five years ago, but I come up here and visit every now and then."

"Texas? What's in Texas?" she asked.

"It's nice out there. The weathers nice, the people nice, it's more opportunity, more jobs, it's just straight out there. If you went down there to one of those clubs, you would get all the dudes. They be all over pretty girls like you."

She smiled, "Thanks. That don't sound too bad, I never thought about moving to Texas. I don't know anyone down there though."

"Well now you know one person. If you trying to get into a certain field, I'll be happy to plug you in with some good people that be about their biz. I'm not trying to sound like I'm the man or anything, but I know some good people."

"Ok, that's cool. I'll keep that in mind," she said, finally seeing that this date wasn't a waste of her time. Sincere and Kiwi was in their own world kissing almost at every red light. Sincere was feeling him and Kiwi was feeling her. Kiwi knew not to play with her because he was already crossing the line just by going behind her dad back so he wasn't going to do anything to become hated.

"So you have any brothers or sisters?" Crews asked.

"Not that I know of, my mom only had me but with my dad there aint no telling how many kids he has."

"You not close to him?"

"No, I really don't know him to be honest but that's another story and I get emotional when I talk about my parents so can we change the subject please?"

Crews noticed her eyes watering just a little so he had no problem changing the story. The last thing he wanted on his first date with her was to have her crying. "No problem. So you have any kids?"

"No, not yet but in a couple years I would like to have one."

"Just one."

"Maybe two," she said, smiling. "Do you have any?"

"I have two, they're by the same woman."

"Oh ok. What do you have?"

"I have a boy that's seven and a girl that's about to turn four next month."

"Dang, you have a seven year old?"

He laughed, "What? That's bad?"

"Naw, I'm just saying. How old are you?"

"Guess."

"No tell me."

"Guess," he said, with a smile.

"25?" she said hoping he wasn't really older than that.

"32, but thanks," he said, and they both laughed. "That's too old for you?"

"No. I always talked to older guys. I just thought you was younger because…" she paused.

"Because what?"

"I don't know, you still got like a young swag about yourself," she said, not really wanting to stroke his ego. Crews just ran his hand across his chin and smiled.

"Yeah, I do I got that swag, don't I?" he joked.

She laughed, "Boy whatever!" she said, cracking up.

"You said it yourself though!"

"I didn't know you was going to be doing all this!" she said, looking at him with a small grin. Then she couldn't help but to smile. "You is not all that!" she joked.

They finally arrived at their destination. They ate there and rode the go karts for about an hour, then they headed to the Michigan State game. Although, they were a little late, their seats were still open. Triangle hadn't been out in so long she didn't want to go home. She was having a ball with Crews, just her and Crews, because Sincere and Kiwi kept sneaking off being nasty with one another. Crews and Triangle was able to talk about whatever and their conversation never went dry.

CHAPTER 34

On their way back home, Triangle was tired but she didn't mind the questions Crews was still asking her. She could tell he liked her just by all his questions. He was fearless with questions.

"So you going home and go to sleep tonight or you going to party some more?"

"I'm tired Crews, I might just fall to sleep at Sincere house," she said.

"How far do you stay from Sincere?"

"I… I stay with my grandmother, but she don't stay far from there, I just don't feel like driving over there."

"When you going to get your own spot?"

"Probably when I save up some money. I have a shopping problem so it be hard for me to save the little money I do get."

"Well how much you get?"

"What, money?"

"Yeah, how much money you make in a month?"

She was caught off guard. "I make ok money, just a couple thousand."

"Oh, ok that's not bad. You have good credit and all that good stuff?"

"Yes," she lied.

"Well why you don't let me help you get a condo or something."

Triangle eyes widen, but she tried to hide it. "A condo?" she asked.

"Yeah, a condo not much. I know where some at for only a thousand a month. I'll pay half and you pay half."

She smiled because it sounded good. "I don't even know you like that Crews."

"I know you don't, but you will see that I'm a good nigga and my intentions is to fuck with you when I come to Michigan."

"Ummm, I don't know about that Crews."

"What? You have nothing to worry about, everything will be in your name, you aint even got to give me a key."

She was quiet, thinking about how bossy she would be with her own Condo. "Where is these Condos located?"

"Right in Auburn Hills. Tomorrow just go to this address," he said, as he pulled out his wallet and gave her a business card for the complex. "Ask for Ryan. He's a good friend of mine. Tell him I sent you. Make sure you have all your paper work so that he can get you right in."

"I'm not ready just yet. I gotta save up a little something before all that. I gotta get furniture and all."

"Leave all that to me. I got you ok," he said, grabbing her hand and kissing it. That made her feel special but she felt like she owed him something.

"What you doing tonight? Where you going?" she asked.

"I'ma go up to my room and get me some sleep," he told her.

"By yourself?"

"Yeah."

"I want to come," she said, smiling.

"I don't mind," he said putting his arm around her and pulling her closer. Sincere had already told Kiwi that Triangle will stay the night so Kiwi was already headed to the hotel room to drop Crews and Triangle off. Triangle

160

noticed that they had arrived right in front of Holiday Inn's front door.

CHAPTER 35

"What we doing here?" she whispered, to Crews.

"I guess they was dropping me off first, but you can come with me," he said, as he opened the door and threw up the peace sign to Sincere and Kiwi.

"Bye yall! Nice meeting you Kiwi, you better be nice to my friend too!" she said, as she was walking in behind Crews.

Triangle walked inside the room and realized he was staying in a presidential suite. It had everything you needed inside.

"Make yourself comfortable. You had a nigga sweating and shit today."

She laughed. "Whatever!" she said, smiling and blushing.

"I'm serious," he said, "Gone ahead and order us a movie to watch."

"I'm coming with you," she said standing up and throwing her purse on the bed and walking over to him.

"In the shower?"

"Yeah, you scared?" she asked.

He looked down at her. "Come on," he said, walking to the bathroom. "You got some extra panties?"

"I didn't wear any."

He smiled, "You something else. Sincere didn't tell me all this."

"All what? You haven't seen nothing yet."

"Ok, ok, well I'm more than happy to assist you," he said, as he started to get undressed. She got undressed as well and Crews couldn't help but check out her body. She had smooth skin and a nice curvy body but he had seen that through her clothes earlier.

"Damn you sexy as hell," he said, eyeing her up and down.

She smiled, "Thank you. You gone turn on the water?"

"Yeah!" he said, making it hot but not too hot. He ran the shower while they both stood there butt naked and as he was making sure it wasn't too hot Triangle smacked him on his butt and made him jump. She burst out laughing.

"Aww hell naw, you can't be doing that Triangle." he said, smiling.

She laughed, "I couldn't help it, it looked soft."

163

"Yeah ok," he said, as he stepped in and she stepped in behind him.

"You wash me and I wash you," she said, as she grabbed the soap and towel.

"Ok, who going first?"

"I'll wash you off first," she said, soaping up the towel. She made sure it was enough soap on the towel then she ran it across his chest and stomach. He didn't have a six or eight pack, but he wasn't fat either, he was buff. She washed each arm slowly but good, then she made her way in between his legs washing his balls and his dick. He was on soft until she begin rubbing the towel and soap all over it. It hardened up.

"Somebody's excited," she said, while washing it with the towel.

He laughed and his dick was sticking straight out. Triangle was a little disappointed because from how tall he was, she thought he would be packing but she was wrong. He was about as long as her middle finger.

"Of course, you touching all over it, what is it supposed to do?"

"I don't know, that's what I'm trying to find out."

"Oh yeah?"

"Yeah," she said, as she dropped to her knees and put his dick in her mouth. She sucked and slobbed over his dick while the water ran over her hair. She was able to put his whole dick in her mouth so that's what she did nonstop. She kept him in her throat while she was twisting her tongue making his body jerk.

"Damn baby," he whispered, realizing she knew what she was doing.

"Ohh shit!" he whispered, and she stopped and started sucking on his balls.

"Why you stop?" he said, as he looked down at her.

"We doing it before you cum nigga."

"I'm about to pop this ex pill," he said

"You do them?"

"Yeah, do you?"

"No, I never have, I always wanted to though."

"I got plenty if you want to get down."

"I'll think about it," she said.

He grabbed her head and started making her suck his dick again. She moaned letting him know she liked his aggressiveness.

She sucked and sucked and stroked him with her hand until he came inside her mouth. She swallowed it with no hesitation.

"Damn, you a lil pro," he said, as he was still jerking while she was sucking the last of his cum from his dick. When she was done she stood on her feet and Crews reached into his pants pocket and grabbed two pills and popped them in his mouth. "You sure?" he said, hugging her then squeezing her wet booty cheeks.

"Yeah, I'ma pass I don't want to be in here acting crazy."

"Alright then."

"Plus I'm still a lil tipsy from the stuff we drinked earlier."

CHAPTER 36

Crews washed her body next and he gave her a small sample of how he was going to eat her pussy when they got out the shower. They dried each other off when they stepped out the shower and Triangle wrapped her hair in a towel.

They both walked to the bed naked and as soon as they got on the bed they went at each other for hours, starting with Crews eating her pussy. He knew what he was doing with his tongue and his dick, so his size didn't really mean much. Plus Triangle had been soaking in vinegar often and her pussy was tight so she felt every bit of him. They fucked until three in the morning before Triangle fell asleep.

Around ten that morning, Crews phone was ringing off the hook. He let it ring the first two times, but whoever was calling wouldn't stop calling so he got up and answered it. "Hello."

"Why you ain't answering the phone?"

"I'm sleep! Why you calling like you crazy?" he said, walking into the bathroom and closing the door. It was Kiwi.

"Cynique got swooped on the way to pick up."

"What you mean on the way?"

"I'm about to pull up right now, come outside and holla at me."

"Alright, here I come," Crews said, putting on his pants and leaving the room.

Triangle had woke up but was still lying in the bed. She wondered what was going on with Crews. She knew it had to be something serious by the way it sounded. She laid in the bed for thirty minutes. Finally Crews came back through the door, Triangle turned over and looked at him. "You ok?"

"Yeah, I'm good. Why what's up?" he said, moving quickly like he was looking for something. She knew he was lying. It was written all over his face.

"You sure?"

"Yeah Triangle, I just gotta find a driver real quick."

"A driver for what?"

"Pick something up for me out of town."

"Where it is?" she asked.

"Actually I need you to come through for me on this. It's a onetime thing and I'ma give you $20,000 for doing it."

That was a lot of money and Triangle was ready but she was wondering what the hell is worth paying $20,000 for. "What is it, if you don't mind me asking?"

"Fifty keys of cocaine."

"Damn," she said, and then she got quiet. She thought about the risk involved, then she thought about how she already worked for the police anyway. If she got caught she could just make another deal with them. "I'll do it, when do you need it done and where I gotta go?"

"ASAP and you gotta go to Texas. They all ready to go. I'll fly you there, and you drive them back."

"I'll do it. When do I get the $20,000?"

"As soon as you get back, I'll tear you right off."

"Deal."

"Get dressed, we gotta go," he said, and she got up. They rushed straight to the airport and Triangle was on the next plane available. All she was thinking about was that $20,000.

CHAPTER 37

Once she arrived in Texas she called Crews and he had her picked up by a Mexican lady. The lady then drove her to the car she was supposed to drive back. It was a Buick Lucerne with a GPS inside. Triangle got in and took off onto the highway. She didn't know whether the dope was in the back seat or in the trunk, but she didn't care. The only thing on her mind was that $20,000. As soon as she got on the highway she called Crews on another number he gave her and he was talking dirty to her for nearly an hour before they hung up.

The next day around noon, Triangle had arrived on a street called Cherry Lawn in Detroit at an address Crews gave her. She called him when she parked inside the garage.

"I'm about to pull up in a second," he told her before he hung up. Triangle became a little nervous when she heard a noise but she figured it was Crews arriving. About two minutes later she seen a door open and it was Crews waving for her to come inside. She got out and walked inside and he hugged and kissed her on the lips. "Thank you so much." He handed her a Louie bag full of money. "It's all there."

"Thank you!" she said, with a big smile. "I need to use the bathroom. Is anyone here?"

"No, just me, hurry up, we got to get out of here."

"Ok, I'm just go brush my teeth real quick," she said, as she got out the travel pack she brought from the gas station.

While she was brushing her teeth, Crews walked in behind her and started feeling on her booty and her pussy.

"I'm dirty right now, stop," she said, with a mouth full of tooth paste. Crews was so happy she got the package back he didn't care how dirty she was. He started pulling her pants down. She still had no panties on. She was wearing the same thing she had been wearing. He leaned her over the sink, while she was still brushing.

"This my pussy now," he said, then he forced his hard dick in her pussy from behind and started stroking her.

"mmm, yes," she moaned.

Crews started pounding her once he felt her pussy get wetter. All you could hear was the counter making a boom noise with each pump. Crews went harder and harder and

Triangle threw her ass back on his dick until he exploded inside her.

A week later Triangle was moving in her Condo. Crews had paid for everything and their relationship was growing stronger by the day. He was making sure he got Triangle attached to him for what he was about to make her a part of. Triangle was falling in love with him, because he was so different from all the other men she had ever met. He was spending money on her for whatever she wanted.

"Well baby, I'll see you in a few weeks," he told her.

"A few weeks, why so long?"

"Texas is where I stay Triangle. I just can't be all laid up with you, I got a girl at home."

"Ok I get it, how many times you gonna throw her up in my face? I know you got a girl and you can keep the bitch, just make time for me."

"I will."

"You can fly me in whenever. I'll take off work to come see you."

"Ok," he said, kissing her on the lips. "When you go back to work?"

"I got two more days off, why?"

"I was gone try to get you out there before you go back."

"Just let me know and I'll come whenever I can. What kind of car you think I should get?" she asked.

"Just get you a lil something, it ain't gotta be that flashy."

"Your car flashy."

He turned and looked at her and smiled, "What that mean?"

"I want a foreign car too."

"Alright, I'll get you something. I should have some mail over here next week, I ordered a big ass safe. I'll pick it up next week sometime. Make sure you sign for it ok? It should be here Tuesday, don't forget."

"I won't boo."

"I'm your boo now huh?" he said, walking out the door.

"You been my boo," she said, smiling running after him. "Wait! Come here," she said, grabbing him and tongue kissing him. She was whipped.

CHAPTER 38

When he left she got on the phone and called Shed.

"Hey, what you doing?"

"Nothing about to leave a friend's house," she lied, not wanting him to know she had a place. She knew Crews would be in and out monthly from her house and she didn't want him getting involved with what she had going on.

"Meet me at my house," he told her. "Remember the guy I was telling you about out of Ohio?"

"Yeah."

"I know I told you after your vacation but I need you right now. Come to my house and I'll tell you more."

"Ok, I'm on my way."

"How long?"

"Give me forty five minutes."

"Fine."

They hung up and Triangle headed over to his house. She didn't mind because she wasn't doing anything else. The only thing she was about to do was go shopping. Soon as she arrived at Detective Shed house she noticed his wife backing out of the driveway. Triangle drove in after she left. His wife didn't like Triangle at all.

"Have a seat real quick," Detective Shed said, while on his laptop. Triangle sat next to him and began looking at his computer screen.

"What you looking up?" she asked.

"The guy in Ohio is leaving Michigan tonight on a flight back to Las Vegas. His name is Red, and I'm trying to get you a seat right next to him on the plane."

"I'm going to Vegas?"

"Kinda, I'm going to send you there to at least get his number, but as soon as you land, you catch the next flight back to Michigan and we are going to try to catch another guy they call Cat."

"Cat, Red, whatsup with all these nick names?"

"They think they're slick that's all."

"So tell me a little about the guys. I read a few things from my folder, but I was really trying to focus on Bonus at the time."

"Ok, Red is a tall light skin guy, around 250 pounds. He's messing with about five kilos of Heroin. He think he's real smooth with it too. He own about ten salons, most of them are in cities all over Ohio, but he has three in Michigan. He's married with four kids and they are all in high school in Cleveland, Ohio. He drives a Ford Explore no rims or nothing. His wife drives a minivan. Now his kids drives 2 Chargers, a Magnum, and a Chrysler 300. He must have a plug at Chrysler. All the cars are registered to Brittany Plotty, my partner is investigating her right now. He loves paying for sex. He has two young girls around 23 and 24 that he deals with. One out of Detroit, her name is Angela Waters. She drives a small Lexus that I think he bought and she works as a bartender. The other girl is from Ohio, her name is Nicole Goins. Beautiful girl, she mixed with Indian and Black. She drives a Mercedes and she works at a bank. My plan is to dress you up so that you appear classy but young. Have you driving a nice car and maybe you can get him to bite."

"Yeah, I got it. I got a plan. What about the other guy because Red sounds a little difficult?"

"Cat! He's another big guy, he has a Marijuana operation. Fucker has a ten bedroom home in a gated community and he grows weed there. He has generators underground."

"What the generators do?"

"They run the lights he has hovering over the plants he is growing. If he didn't have generators his electric bill would be thousands a month."

"He seems kind of smart, how did you find out about this guy?"

"Well he's been doing what he's doing for a while, but I got on to him because his generators take gas, and he's the dummy that goes and buys it. I seen him one day filling up three big containers of gas and I just figured I'll follow him to see where all this gas is going. He went to the house and I waited hours for him to leave again. A week later I set up a construction site nearby, and found out this guy has generators built at least fifteen feet underground."

"Why so deep?"

"The ones he have are loud, but after diggin so far, we were not able to hear them."

"Damn, that's crazy, so how you knew what it was for?"

"We know guys he deals with and they sell weed. We have done some traffic stops on him and caught him before with thirty to forty pounds of Exotic weed. Kush is what they call it on the streets. He did five years back in 2000. He will be easy for you though, he owns a strip club in Detroit on 8 mile and the word is he sleeps with all his employees. So all you have to do is get a job up there, and be different from the other girls and bingo, we in. We can get him, but as you know since I'm federal, I like to hit hard as I can hit."

CHAPTER 39

Triangle smiled, "What's the biggest guy you ever caught?"

"Aww shit, I den got guys with tons of Cocaine, truckloads of weed, busloads of heroin. Those are the big boy's. I'm working on a case right now out of California, this guy is a multimillionaire and he moves thousands of Kilos of Cocaine. I'm this close to nailing this guy on a conspiracy charge."

"Why don't I got the guys like that?"

"You have to work your way up. Right now, these type of guys is a lot smarter and I don't want anything bad to happen to you. Once you get skilled better, you will be. Trust me, but for now, I'm going to send you on this flight. As soon as you get back I want you to go apply for a job at his strip club, then—"

"Wait, I'm not stripping. I'll be a bartender or something. I know people in Detroit."

"You're not even 21, you can't serve drinks. Apply as a stripper."

"I'm not doing that."

"Well you're going to jail."

"What the hell is that Shed! This is bullshit!" she stood up turning red in the face.

"It's your job Triangle. Shit is going to get way crazier than this. You rather go to prison for the rest of your life or you want to be a stripper for a couple months? You act like I asked you to fuck twenty guys on camera."

Triangle sat down and was thinking, she was pissed and she didn't want to do this. She thought about her uncle and her grandmother and how they would feel about her. It hit her again and she was mad at her life. She was so mad she was involved in this situation. She wanted out and she had barely even started yet. She seen that Detective Shed wasn't a friend to her, this was all about catching these drug dealers and putting them away.

Two hours later Triangle was stepping on the flight to Vegas. The airport was jam packed. She was nervous and scared, but ready. She knew she had to pull herself together.

Finally she made it to her seat and Red was right there sitting. "I think this is where I'm supposed to be, I'm not sure though, this my first time flying," she lied, smiling, showing her pretty teeth.

Red eyed her and was instantly attracted to her. "Let me see your ticket," he said, as she handed it to him and he read it. "Yup, your seat is right here. Don't worry though, I'm cool and laid back, I won't bother you," he said, with a smile.

"Where should I put this bag?" He got up and put it above them. "Thank you so much."

"You welcome, I'm Red," he said, sticking out his hand for her to shake.

"I'm Triangle."

"Triangle? That's an uncommon name."

"I'm an uncommon girl," she said, not wasting any time with him. She got her flirt on right away.

"How old are you? If you don't mind me asking, because you look a lil young."

"I'm 18."

"18? Wow, you are young. You going to Vegas by yourself?"

"I'm going to visit my uncle, he stays there. I haven't seen him in like a year."

"Oh ok, you really never been on a plane before huh? I can tell from your body language."

"I look nervous? Oh my god," she said, turning red in the face.

"I use to be married to a Detective, she taught me a lil something." he said, with a smile.

She turned his way and crossed her legs and swung her hair back, "What is my body saying now?"

He laughed, "You silly, you been drinking?"

"A little, but shh, don't say that too loud, they might kick me off the plane or move my seat."

"Naw you good sweetheart, I won't get you moved."

"Oh so you want me to stay?"

"Look at you, I see you're very outspoken."

"I mean, I'm young but I go for what I want."

"So it's like that."

"Yeah."

Red felt as if he lucked up finding him another young freak. He was all for it too, and wasn't letting her out his sight before getting her contact information, he had to have her.

"How long you going to be staying in Vegas?" he asked.

"How long do you want me to stay?"

"Ohh wee, I like you. They sat me next to the right person," he said, smiling. "Talking like that, you must trying to come chill with me?"

"I could, that wouldn't be a problem. How long are you going to be in Vegas?"

"A few weeks."

"I can't stay that long, I got money to get back too," she said.

"You got money to get back too? Where you work?" he asked.

"I don't work."

"So you just get money without working?"

"I got people working for me."

"Oh you own your own business?"

"Something like that, I have a little hustle going on."

"Hustling what? Shoes and clothes?"

She laughed, shaking her head no.

"Don't tell me you be selling drugs, you too pretty to be doing that."

"Thanks for the compliment."

"You welcome," he said wondering why she didn't answer his question. "You be selling drugs?"

"Don't tell me you the police," she said.

He laughed, "Hell naw girl, I been to prison twice."

"I do a little something," she said.

"What you mess with?"

"Heroin."

"Heroin? Seriously?" he asked shockingly.

"Yeah, I just started though, I'm only getting a few ounces," she said.

"A few ounces is good for you. I can't believe you fucking with Heroin. I woulda never guessed that what it was. You know what you doing with that?"

"I know a lil something. Is that what you went to prison for?"

"Once yeah, I did seven years for Heroin. I just came home about three years ago."

"You still dealing with it?"

He was quiet for a second, "Well, I got people. Actually we can exchange numbers and I'll hook you up with one of my mans and he'll hook you up with a better price and better shit."

"I'm not trying to meet no one messing with this stuff. It's too many people telling out here, not saying your boy is a snitch, but you know what I mean."

Red smiled, "You funny, I like your style. I wont introduce you to him then, since you don't want no one knowing what you do. That's smart, always be like that. I'm go still take care of you though, don't even worry. If you tryna mess with it on a bigger scale I got you, but keep that on the hush."

"I will, you don't have to worry about that," she said.

"Is your uncle picking you up from the airport?"

"If I call him he will, but I was just going to catch a cab."

"Well, later after you see him, you need to come up to my room and kick it with me. You smoke and drink?"

"Yeah, I'll come, I drink a little, and I don't want to smoke though."

"That's cool, you don't have to, I was just asking." Red was happy, he had found him another young chick who he was about to put on his team. He had never met a girl this young that was doing what Triangle said she was doing. He wanted to help her.

CHAPTER 40

They arrived at the airport and Triangle left with Red telling him she would catch up with her uncle later. They talked more and got to know each other more, and all Red was thinking about was fucking her. She was a total package, Red was going to do whatever she wanted him to do. He was ready to spend whatever on her. They got to the hotel room about 7 a.m. and they had been talking and sipping Ace of Spades for three hours now. It was ten o' clock. "You not even go call your uncle and let him know you made it?"

"I been texted him earlier," she lied.

"Oh ok, he was cool?"

"Yeah, he don't care, I had told him I was coming to have fun. I didn't realize how nice it was down here."

"Yeah, and we on the strip where everything is at, if you want to go out let me know, I'll take you and show you around."

"Ok, I'm straight though, I like your company."

"You do? That's what's up. You must like older guys huh?"

"Yes, I always wanted an older guy, but they always said I was too young or they were married. I just know yall know what yall doing."

"Yeah you right about that. I'm glad I met you, you fine as hell," he said, shaking his head while she was sitting on the bed with her legs crossed.

"Thank you," she said, getting up and walking over to where he was sitting. She sat on his lap and put her arm around him.

"Oh ok then. You something else."

"Am I too much?" she asked, looking down at him.

"Naw you good," he said. She was all over him. He was getting suspicious about her, and what her intentions were, he had dealt with plenty of young chicks, but this one was different. He wondered if she was trying to set him up to get robbed or steal from him. At first it was cool, but she was starting to do too much, but he knew what to do. He was just going to watch her closely and see if she was willing to have sex with him tonight. His mind was just wondering around because something this good had never just fallen into his lap before.

As he was thinking and puffing on his blunt, she was still sitting on his lap, now beginning to slowly grind to the music that the commercial on TV was playing. He was quiet. "What's wrong? What you thinking about?"

"Nothing really."

"Yes you are, be honest."

"You just so young, I'm wondering if I'm making a mistake."

"See, I knew you was going to do this," she said, getting off his lap. "You just like the rest, how are you making a mistake?"

"I'm sorry I didn't mean to say that, I'm over thinking shit, this weed got me gone," he said, as he followed her to the bed. "I'm sorry ok, I ain't trying to be categorized with them other niggas you dealing with. It's just I'm really trying to fuck with you on a long term tip."

"And I'm trying to fuck with you too Red. What's the problem?"

Red didn't want to answer that, he wanted to tell her what his gut was telling him, which was to leave her alone, but he just kept it to himself. "Ok, we'll see where things could go, I just hope you not crazy."

She laughed, "I know you got a wife, I don't care about that."

Red just looked at her admiring her beauty. "You a fine ass muthfucka, you know that?"

She shook her head up and down knowing he was about to make a move on her and she didn't care. At this point it was whatever. She knew whatever was about to happen she was going to do her best. She laughed inside her head because Detective Shed thought this mission was going to be hard for her, but it was the opposite, she couldn't wait to tell him. She was going to text him later tonight.

"Look at these lil sexy thighs," he said, rubbing on her softly, she just let him as she sat there looking sexy. Red had to at least be forty years old. He was a big guy and you could tell money was nothing to him. He continued to rub her thighs through her pants then he started rubbing her pussy after she spread her legs for him. "Hhmm." She moaned tilting her head back.

He noticed she was enjoying his touch so he started to unbutton her pants. She didn't stop him, she helped him pull them down. "No panties huh?"

She smiled, "I don't like to wear them much."

"That's sexy," he said, as he threw her pants on the floor. He looked at her pussy and it was nicely shaved with a small hair strip about as skinny as a Newport cigarette. "Look at this pussy here," he said, before he kissed it then began licking it and fingering her.

"Red, oh baby," she moaned lying on her back with her legs spread.

"Damn that pussy taste clean," he told her as he started sticking his long tongue in and out her pussy. He ate her out for nearly an hour, and she came hard twice.

After he was done, she returned the favor and gave him head and rode his dick then she fell asleep on top of him forgetting to even text Detective Shed back.

He had her lying on him, she had sucked his dick, and he had fucked her and nutted in her and his dick was still inside her as she was now sleeping. He was making plans already. He couldn't wait to take her shopping in the morning. He wanted her wearing the best. To him, she was a top notch chick already, but by the time he added his touch she would really be the shit.

CHAPTER 41

Triangle woke up around three in the morning and started sucking his dick until it became hard again, then she started riding him again making herself cum first then him, then fell back to sleep. Red was really loving her, he could tell she loved sex, but so did he, so it was perfect.

Four days later Triangle was on a flight back to Michigan. She had Red eating out the palm of her hands. He had took her shopping two days in a row spending a few thousands on her. She had all the top designer clothes. The whole flight back she was thinking about Crews and what he was doing. She had texted him yesterday but she was ready to see him. He was the one she now loved and he was who she wanted to see. Detective Shed was proud of her and he knew Cat would be even easier for her.

When she landed in Michigan a car was waiting for her. Detective Shed had got her a rental. She drove straight to Cat's strip club and applied for a job. She had no problem getting hired, they started her the next day, and she was now dancing for money butt naked. She went and took pole lessons on the side which was only a one week class that was taught by a lady that knew minor tricks. Triangle learned what she could learn and used it. She had started liking the attention she got from the guys and they were loving her.

One night after everyone was leaving the club, Cat walked her to the Lexus land cruiser Crews had got for her. "Where you going tonight?" he asked.

"With you," she said, smiling. She had been watching him watch her for some days now and she already knew it wouldn't be long before he pushed up on her. She wasn't going to play hard to get either, she was going to give in as if she was a groupie.

"You ain't saying nothing. You riding with me or you want to follow me?"

"Follow you where? Not to a hotel, I don't do hotels. If you don't have a house to take me to you're not worth fucking with anyway," she said, as she got inside her SUV.

He laughed, "I got plenty of houses, let's go. Lock your doors and ride with me," he told her. Triangle was looking sexy, she was wearing some black high heels and a black short dress that looked like a shirt. The sleeves relaxed on her shoulders showing her soft clear skin and her back hung out. Her ass was nearly crawling from under the dress and the black thong was visible every three steps she took. She continued to pull her dress down every time it raised. Cat walked her over to his Range Rover and they were on their way to one of his houses.

He took her to Birmingham, he owned a condo in the downtown area that he had up for sale, but he had furniture and some clothes there.

"So what took you so long to get at me?" she asked, smiling. "I seen you looking at me the first day I worked."

"I like to first know who I'm dealing with before I just make my move. You know it's so many diseases and shit out here. I be trying to watch myself. That's why I make every girl at my club take a HIV test before they work."

"Did you my get my test back yet?" she asked.

"Yeah I got it earlier today I got it in my back pocket. I'll get it when we stop. You good. If you woulda been dirty I woulda fired you."

She laughed, "Why you let me start so fast then before you knew I was clean?"

"Because you fine, I had to get that extra money. I knew my customers was waiting on a face like you to come through, so I made an exception."

"Well thank you, I needed that money anyway."

"Look like you need nothing. You look like your doing great."

"No, I'm ok though."

"So I got a pole at home, you gonna put a show on for me before you give me that pussy?"

Triangle smiled, "Who said I was giving you some pussy?"

"It's almost three o' clock, I know you ain't come to my house this late to not give me none. If so you might as well get out right here and start walking," He told her while pulling over.

"Damn nigga," she said, looking at him like he was crazy.

A month later Triangle was buying 75 pounds a week from Cat. They were still fucking and he was sprung. He was giving her thousands at a time, each time she worked. Sometimes he would call her into his back office to give a personal dance for him and his friends. They didn't throw one dollar bills at her, they threw hundreds and fifties, then he would put them out and fuck her on his pool table. The only thing Triangle didn't like was that he wanted too much of her time. He was trying to take her out on dates and out of town every week until she finally told him she couldn't do that all the time. It wasn't long before he tried to get her to move in with him at the condo in Birmingham. He told her she wouldn't have to pay anything, but she passed. She just took the money he gave her. She needed time to spend with Crews and Red too.

CHAPTER 42

Triangle was knocked out cold at her home when she heard Crews come in. She hadn't seen him in a while but she was excited to see him. He hopped into bed with her, nearly smothering her with his body.

"Stop playing," she said, hitting him on his back.

"Come here, I miss YOU!"

"I miss you too! Where you been? You've been gone a long time!"

"The real question is, have you been keeping that pussy tight for me?"

Triangle just nodded her head at him and slung back the covers for him to climb in beside her.

"Let me see," he said, as he started taking his khaki pants off. He fucked her for about an hour, then he jumped in the shower.

"Your package came too. I know what the hell you having sent here too. You didn't have to lie to me!" she said, yelling into the bathroom, through the steam from his hot shower.

She heard him laugh from inside which only made her madder. "It's not funny Crews!"

"Why you open my shit up?"

"Because I thought you said it was a safe. I was going to get rid of the packaging stuff, but instead I open it and you have five kilos inside. Not cool!"

"Shut up! I ain't got no driver right now. Plus I'm looking out for you, why are you complaining?"

"Don't tell me to shut up! All I'm saying is you could of told me. It makes me wonder what else you lying about? And I ain't complaining, you do take care of me, but for me to take care of you, I gotta know you're being one hundred with me!"

"I'm sorry I lied to you okay. Hey, did you get that money I sent you last week to buy your granny a car?" he asked, changing the subject a little before she had him promising not to lie to her again.

"Yes, I did! She was so happy you should have been there to see the look on her face. Thank you boo!"

"You're welcome! What you get her?"

"I just got her one of those G8 cars by Pontiac. She had a hundred and one questions too. How you get this money?

What you doing? You better not be doing nothing nasty with them boys!" Triangle said, laughing.

"Oh, you doing something nasty alright. What did you tell her?"

"I told her that my boyfriend makes a lot of money! She told me to take care of you and not let you go! I think she would have given you some booty too!"

"Shit, if her pussy like yours run that shit! Hey, I seen your girl Sincere about an hour ago. Her and Kiwi was going to get breakfast."

"Boy you're the nasty one!" she said referring to what he said about her Grandma. "Must be nice for her, I wish I could get someone to take me to breakfast!"

"We do that sometimes, don't act like that girl!"

"Whatever!" Triangle said, sitting on the floor outside the bathroom door when he came out, already dressed.

"Well I gotta go! Where them bricks at?"

"In the closet. That shit strong too. It gave me a headache!"

"What closet?"

"The one in the living room. You really gottta go? You just got here!"

"Yeah I gotta go and get rid of this shit."

"I love you! When you coming back?"

Distracted he said, "Yeah, okay!" not really hearing what she said.

"Oh, you can't say it back to me?"

"What? Oh my bad, damn I love you too Triangle!"

"Well you ain't gotta say it like that! You don't love me, that's okay. I still love you!"

"What the hell is your problem? You been all over me since I got here! Don't be one of those nagging housewives where the man don't even want to come home! You want some more dick or something? You know your position. I do all you want me to do for you and you gonna pull this shit on me?"

Realizing she went too far Triangle back pedaled and apologized, "Okay Crews, I'm sorry! I'll play my position, fuck it!"

"Fuck what?"

"Nothing! It's like you come here, fuck me and then you're gone. We don't go out to dinner or nothing. Where did all the romance go?"

"Look bitch this aint no romance novel! I buy you everything you want. I can't be your man right now!"

"It's not all about money! I don't give a fuck about money! Or what you buy me. I was fine with what I had before you," she said, starting to cry. She ran to the bathroom and tried to close the door, but he followed behind. He hugged and kissed her while they were facing the mirror, until she calmed down. He didn't want her to turn on him or anything, so he had to make it right before he left out the door.

After twenty minutes of calming her down, they ended up in the shower fucking again. He ate her pussy as the water cascaded down her body and she forgot about why she was mad at him.

CHAPTER 43

Crews left with all the dope. Triangle was getting dressed when she heard a knock at the door. "Who is it?" she asked through the door. Cursing herself for not getting a peep hole installed.

"UPS!" Came the reply from the other side of the door.

Damn, another package, she thought to herself. She opened the door and three guys rushed her, knocking her to the floor, tied her up and put a piece of duct tape over her mouth. She looked up and saw all three of them were dark skinned, with big ass shot guns pointed at her with ski masks on.

"I'm gonna take the tape off but if you scream I'm gonna blow your fuckin' wig off bitch!" one of them said, cocking his gauge.

Triangle shook her head to indicate she understood. The other two guys were ransacking her place, looking for whatever they had come for. Probably drugs or money, maybe both. But besides what she had in her purse, there was nothing there. "Bitch where the money at?"

"I don't know! Please don't kill me!" she cried out, hoping for mercy.

"Call that nigga and tell him we got his bitch and she dead if he don't come up with a quarter mil!"

The shortest of the three guys grabbed her phone and hit Crew's number on speed dial. Crews answered right away thinking it was her.

"What's up Triangle?"

"This aint your bitch nigga! She dead unless you come up with a quarter million!"

"What? Get off my phone nigga' and quit playing games!" he said, hanging up on them. The guys questioned Triangle about Crews and where he was getting the dope.

"Let's get out of here for this nigga sends the police over here or something!"

Minutes later they were walking out, dragging Triangle along in broad daylight.

She was still tied up and being held at gun point. They put her inside a van and drove her to a house that was abandoned. Triangle was scared and started praying that they wouldn't kill her.

Once they got settled in and they had Triangle sitting in a chair and they called Crews again, this time from another number.

As soon as Crews answered, the big guy said, "Yeah Nigga!" as he put Triangle up to the phone.

"Help Crews please! They gonna kill me!" she screamed into the phone.

Grabbing the phone back he said, "You thought I was playing games? I got your bitch Triangle! If you want this bitch alive you better bring us a quarter million to--"

Crews cut him off and said, "Fuck you and that bitch! You can have her, nigga catch me if you can!" Crews said, laughing into the phone just before breaking his.

"Naw this nigga didn't?" one of them said, holding the dead phone in his hand.

"What?" the other two asked.

"This nigga said fuck us and that bitch and hung up!"

The other ones started laughing and said, "This must not be his main bitch!"

"Please don't kill me! I'll give you whatever you want. I have a little money saved up for college," she pleaded with them. "I have nothing to do with Crews. He was getting stuff shipped to my house and paying me to hold it. I didn't know what he was doing I swear! We aint nothing that's why he's not coming to my rescue," she cried and reasoned with them. "I'm so sorry. I can pay you though. And I won't say a word I promise!" Triangle said, she was hurt that Crews was leaving her for dead. She really loved him too. She thought he loved her!

"How much money you got bitch?"

"I have like $60,000 saved up!"

"In that house? I didn't see nothing!"

"No, somewhere else. It's at a hotel," she said. She was going to give them the marked money she had. "It might be more than that. But whatever it is, you can have. Just please don't kill me!" Triangle begged as tears fell down her cheeks.

"Alright bitch, where we gotta go?"

She told them and they headed to the hotel Shed had set her up in. Triangle was nervous and she was hoping Shed was there just in case they had plans on killing her anyways. She hadn't seen their faces, but enough through the ski mask, enough to maybe identify them if she saw them again.

CHAPTER 44

When they arrived at the hotel Triangle said, "This place is under surveillance. The feds are watching, so untie me first. You see that car on the corner?" she asked pointing to a blue sedan.

"Yeah, who is it? Is this some kind of trick bitch?"

"It's not a trick. They are federal agents, but just relax. One of you walk up to the room to get the money and you'll be straight!"

They looked at each other, trying to figure out if she was telling the truth, then the bigger one pointed to the guy sitting closest to Triangle and said, "You go with her and lose the ski mask."

They untied her and they walked up to the room together, no ski mask and no gun out. When she got into the room, she handed him the duffel bag and he walked out. She called downstairs to the agents in the lobby right after he left and all three guys were pulled over and caught with the money and taken to jail for armed robbery and kidnapping.

Triangle was heated, she had to get away for a while. Red was right there when she called and they were on their way back to Vegas three days after the incident. Triangle even told Detective Shed about Crews, Kiwi and Sincere's dad selling drugs, she was tired of waiting for people to screw her over or disappoint her. With that info, Shed was able to put cases on Kiwi, Crews and Sincere's dad. Come to find out they were all part of a black cartel out of California, which tied them to the other guy Shed was after as well. Triangle had done a great job and no one had a clue that she was behind the arrest.

She still hadn't bought from Red yet. He didn't want her to sell dope, he was willing to buy her anything she wanted, but she kept trying to get him to sell her something and that made him suspicious.

"What's your last name?" he asked her out of the blue one day, catching her off guard.

"Slate, why?" she asked, giving him a false name.

"Triangle Slate? I was just wondering, I realized I never knew it," he said, playing it off, but really he wanted to have her checked out. There was something not quite right with her, he just couldn't put his finger on it, but he would find out. He loved fucking her and being around her, but he also knew she was hiding something and he needed to know what it was.

"Come on, you asked for a reason!"

"I just wanted to know, that's all. Now come over here and suck daddy's dick," he commanded her, as he lay back on the bed, naked, while puffing on a cigar. Triangle being obedient, went over and began serving him up. They did have fun together, but in the back of her head she was wondering why he wanted her name. Red picked up his video camera and started filming her naked. She let him have his way because she thought that would make them close, but Red was smarter than that.

A week later they flew back to Michigan and Red had already called his ex-wife, the one who used to be a detective, she was waiting to tail Triangle.

Detective Shed had been calling her all week and she knew as soon as she arrived, she would have to go over there and give him some pussy so that they wouldn't be beefing.

Red walked her to a cab and gave her a hug goodbye and said, "Call me baby!"

"Okay, I will!" she said, as he closed the door behind her and she waved goodbye to him. "Wow, I've never seen a black lady cab driver before. How you doing?" Triangle asked as the driver got going and headed for the airport exit.

"I'm good and you?" Red's ex-wife asked her.

Triangle had no clue who she was. "I'm good, just got back off a nice trip with a friend."

"How was it girl?"

"It was really good!"

"That's good. Where do you want to go?"

"Saginaw! I have to check in with my boss."

"What kind of work you do?" she asked, looking in the rear view mirror.

"I just do minor law work," Triangle said, not getting into details.

"Minor law work? Like what, a lawyer? I used to be a detective for years!"

"Really? Well you must know Detective Shed?"

"Yes! That was my partner of three years. What a small world. How do you know him?"

"He's my boss. I'm going in to report to him."

"Wow! This is crazy! I can't believe your boss is my old partner. What kind of shit he got you doing girl? Was you working on the trip you just came from?" she asked, probing a little further and harder.

"Yeah, I almost got this guy right where I want him, but he ain't went the whole nine yards yet!"

"Damn, you just a young thing, you can't be a detective already. You one of Sheds informants?"

"Y..Yeah!" Triangle stuttered, surprised she guessed it right.

"It's okay. I've worked with many informants in the past. What's he got you into girl if you don't mind me asking?"

"Just busting down drug dealers, nothing spectacular! It's pretty easy actually!"

"What kind of case he had on you? I know he's a scandalous cop, he only cares about arrests!"

Triangle began to feel a little uncomfortable telling her all this. "Um, I'm not supposed to tell anyone, but between you and me, murder!"

"Wow, you got off pretty good then. Just make sure he don't string you out too long baby girl!" Red's ex-wife said, getting everything she said on a tape recorder, she couldn't wait to tell Red and collect the few thousands he paid her for her services.

Triangle had the cab drop her off at Shed's house and then he drove them to the hotel. Triangle gave him some head on the drive over, because she knew he was mad at her.

A week later her phone woke her up ringing like crazy. It was a private number, but she answered, "Hello?"

"Bitch you dead!" was all she heard and they hung up immediately.

Then the phone rang right back, "Hellooo?" she asked into the receiver.

"Snitch ass bitch!!"

The phone hung up again and now she was wide awake. She wondered who knew she was telling. Then the phone rang again, this time it was Sincere number.

"Hello Sincere, what's up girl?"

"My dad is gone!" she cried into the phone.

CHAPTER 45

Triangle's Uncle Phillip, daughters Julie and Jacky were walking his mom to her car and his wife was standing in the doorway waving goodbye. Julie and Jacky were in town for a couple of days, before they headed back to college. They were enjoying the time they were spending with their mom and dad. They hadn't seen them in months.

"This the car Triangle bought for you?" Phillip asked, smiling.

"Yeah, that girl done got me this fast thing! I like it though," his mom said, laughing.

They all laughed with her as Julie asked with surprise, "Triangle bought you this? What she doing to make this kind of money?"

"Yeah really!" Jacky chimed in.

"I'm not sure, but she has a Lexus and some other car too!" Phillip told them.

"I'm Jealous!" Jacky said out loud.

Phillip walk his mom to her car and hugged and kissed her. "Bye mom, drive safe!"

A black van crept up the street while he was opening her car door. It stopped. It had black tinted windows that slowly rolled down, and a big steel barrel pointed out.

"Get down!" Phillip yelled, as he pushed his mom inside the car and then ran towards his girls. The van door slid open and more gunshots rang out.........

*****

"What do you mean he's gone?"

"The police came and got him!"

"Oh my God Sincere. That's horrible. I'm so sorry! Where are you?"

"I'm at home!"

"I'm on my way girl, stay there!" she said, hanging up and racing over there for her friend. She honked her horn as soon as she was in her driveway and Sincere came running out.

Sincere got in the car and Triangle asked, "What happened?"

"The feds indicted them all, including Kiwi! There was like fourteen defendants in all. I told him to stop, and that we had enough money!" she cried.

"Damn, that shit is messed up!" Triangle said, driving to Detroit to get something to eat. She knew it was her fault. The least she could do is buy her something to fill her stomach. They went to a fancy restaurant downtown.

"I've never been here before."

"Oh it's nice, trust me. I wouldn't even waste your time. They have some good soul food here."

"I don't really have a appetite, but I'll snack on something."

"Yeah, eat something it will make you feel better girl," she said, as she watched Sincere walk ahead of her and grab a flyer off the wall, she was reading it when Triangle walked up and both of their eyes grew big as apples.

After Sincere was done reading it she slapped Triangle across the face as hard as she could.

"You dirty bitch!" Sincere shouted, as she rushed at her, slamming her into the wall. Triangle fell to the ground. Sincere followed that up by punching Triangle in the mouth.

"Wait! Let me explain," Triangle said, blocking the next punch.

"Fuck you bitch, you can't explain this," Sincere said, rolling the flyer up and stuffing it in Triangles mouth. Then she stood up and kicked Triangle in the face and chest.

There were people walking past, reading the same flyer. They were put up all over the place. Nobody stopped Sincere from beating Triangle. When she was done she left out and couldn't stop crying. She wanted to kill Triangle and she couldn't wait to talk to her dad. She was in shock that she had just read a flyer with Triangles face on it. There was five small pics on it: One where she was naked. One where she was sucking a dick, another where she was at the club dressed to impress and another naked one. It said she was an informant for the FEDS and she had told on a lot of people, her dad included.

Whoever made the flyers had to have money because they were posted up all over the city. Triangle had ratted on Crew's, Kiwi, her dad, Bonus, Cat and a couple of other dealers. Triangles phone was ringing off the hook from everyone she knew about her working for the FEDS. She was getting all kind of death threats.

As Sincere was riding in the cab she got a call from her dad. He was calling collect and she accepted the charges.

The first thing he said was, "Leave that bitch Triangle alone! She aint right!"

"I know, I just beat that bitch's ass! She told on you! I should have listened when you told me before to leave her alone!"

"I know, I know. Don't worry though, I'ma take care of it. Don't touch her anymore while this shit is going on, okay?"

"Okay daddy! You alright in there?"

"Yeah I'm good. Make sure you come see me tomorrow, we gotta talk!"

"Okay, call me back later, my phone is going dead. I love you!" Sincere said, as her phone started beeping indicating a low battery.

"I love you too baby!" he said as the phone shut off.

CHAPTER 46

Triangle was all bloody as she stumbled to her car. No one helped her, in fact they started throwing stuff at her, soda cans, glass beer bottles, soda bottles, rocks and anything else they could get their hands on. They were all screaming at her calling her a snitch and rat! A piece of cheese hit her in the back of the head, as they chanted, "Ratt Bitttch!" One girl ran up on her and started punching her in the back of the head, knocking her to the ground again. Crawling and stumbling she made it to her car. She started it up and nearly ran a bunch of people over in the process of getting away. She backed into a car, wrecking her back end as she escaped. Suddenly, shots rang out from both sides of her car, blowing her windows out and thudding into her doors. The only glass not shot out was the windshield. Vans chased and shot at her until she was out of sight. She raced across the freeway at a hundred and something all the way to the hotel. She called Shed and told him what had happened and he was on the way to meet her. In her mind she could hear her uncle advising her about the life lessons he tried to instill in her. Her nose was bleeding, quite possibly broken and she wanted to run away. She had money stashed and she wanted to leave the state after she talked to Shed.

When she pulled into the hotel parking lot she saw a pair of black vans, just like the ones that had chased her. As soon as they seen her drive in, they were on her, shooting through their windows. She did a U-turn and headed back on the highway, heading to Sheds house. She called him again and turned him around. He called the police to block off the highway so no one could chase her and get her there safely. He also reported the black vans to the dispatcher.

Triangle made it to his house safe and sound, but she was shaking and crying when she arrived. "I'm done!" she said falling into his arms.

"Calm down! What's going on?"

"They know!" was all she said.

"How?" he asked.

"I don't know how they know, but they know!"

Shed shook his head at the turn of events. He knew how dangerous this could get when drug lords found out there was a snitch and especially when they found out the identity of the snitch. He had to protect Triangle and being in Michigan was not safe for her.

"We gotta get out of here. I'ma take you to the airport. It's not safe here either," he said, moving fast. He had no idea what Triangle had done, but he was getting calls on his phone as well saying he was dead. Red knew everything about Triangle and Shed. His ex-wife had told him everything. As soon as they came out of Sheds house, Triangle heard two shots go off and felt them pierce her arm and lower stomach area. She heard more shots ring out and then she fell to the ground. "Get down!" Shed yelled at Triangle before he was hit four times.

Triangle screamed but she was quieted by a hail of gunfire that exploded her head and chest cavity. The smoking shells hit the ground as the vans peeled rubber, fleeing the scene in broad daylight. Shed and Triangle lay in blood puddles, no longer moving or breathing.

Every drug dealer Triangle had busted went to trial and beat the case due to lack of evidence and witnesses. Sincere dad and Crews got out. Red had contacted all of them and told them not to take the plea deal the prosecutors were offering them because he had everything covered. Even the officers Shed had called to block the highway for Triangle was working for Red's ex-wife so they never showed up to the call. Red was just a five kilo buying guy, but after he put that play down, he jumped in with Sincere's dad and he was getting 20 to 50 kilos of heroin at a time. Shed and Triangle were pronounced dead at the scene. Phillip was paralyzed from the waist down, his wife didn't get hit, but his daughters did. They were both in critical condition. The Grandmother was shot fourteen times and was pronounced dead at the scene as well.

In trying to get her life right, Triangle ruined everyone else's. She died at 18, her last conscious thought, was that finally they would leave her alone.....

Other books by the Author

Women Lie Men Lie part 1

Women Lie Men Lie part 2

Women Lie Men Lie part 3

Stack Before Your Splurge

Please, Please, Please leave a review about how you feel about the book.

https://www.amazon.com/A-Roy-Milligan/e/B009YEVZPC?ref=sr_ntt_srch_lnk_2&qid=1587560927&sr=8-2